HEAVEN SENT HUSBAND

GILBERT MORRIS

Steeple
Hill®

Published by Steeple Hill·Books™

STEEPLE HILL BOOKS

Steeple
Hill®

RECYCLED PAPER

ISBN 0-373-87308-5

HEAVEN SENT HUSBAND

Copyright © 2005 by Gilbert Morris

www.SteepleHill.com

Printed in U.S.A.

Without faith, it is impossible to please Him, for he that cometh to God must believe that He is, and that He is a rewarder of them that diligently seek Him.

—*Hebrews* 11:6

To Johnnie—my companion for fifty-six years.
I've enjoyed every second of it!

·GILBERT MORRIS

makes his home in Gulf Shores, Alabama, with his wife, Johnnie. He was a Baptist pastor for twenty years, a professor of English for twenty-eight years and since retiring, he has written 186 novels. He is involved in prison ministry in Alabama and Florida.

Ket turned casually and then suddenly froze.

The sight of the tall man who had just entered the cafeteria had an almost paralyzing effect on her.

"Now, *he* is something!" Debbie breathed. "Did you ever see a better-looking man in your whole life?"

The man they were staring at was six foot five, with a lean, athletic-looking build. He had auburn hair, light blue eyes and strong, even features. Ket's friends, Maggie and Debbie, watched with shock as he suddenly turned toward them and smiled.

"Do you know him?" Maggie whispered.

Ket had no time to answer for the tall man stopped before them and looked down at her. "Hello, Ket," he said.

"Hello, Jared. It's nice to see you again."

Ket's friends looked at them in stunned silence. "Who was that?" Maggie gasped as he walked away.

"When I think of Jared Pierce, all I can remember is a rather nasty boy who teased me about being so tall. He was always pulling my ponytail, and once he pushed me into a mud puddle."

Debbie grinned. "He could push me into the Atlantic Ocean!"

Chapter One

Ketura Lindsey took a firm grip on the squirming bundle of fur she held in her right arm. The whiskered face of the Yorkie looked up at her eagerly. "Now, Bedford," she said, "you're going to have to behave yourself. This is a hospital and you're going to meet a very sick, young man. So you must be very good."

Passing through the front door of Mercy Hospital, Ket smiled at the silver-haired woman behind the desk in the center of the room. "What's that you've got there?" the woman asked cheerfully.

"This is my good buddy Bedford. I'm taking him up to see Denny Ray."

"Did you get Dr. Bjelland's permission for that?"

"No." Ket smiled. "I'm smuggling him in. You won't tell on me, will you, Mrs. Williams?"

Mrs. Williams smiled and shook her head. She had a special fondness for Ket Lindsey and she studied the young woman before she answered. Ket had ash-blond hair and blue-gray eyes set in a squarish face. Her fair complexion was marked with a few, almost invisible freckles. She was very tall, just under six feet. There was a strength in her and her face was marked by this strength rather than beauty.

"No. I won't squeal. Here, let me say hello. Hi, Bedford." She reached out and petted the head of the frantically wiggling dog who tried to get at her face. "No—no, you can't lick my face! All this makeup would make you sick." She laughed. "Go on up. Denny Ray will be glad to see you."

Moving out of the main lobby, Ket took the elevator up to the fourth floor. Passing by the nursing station, she stopped long enough to say, "Hello, Ellie. I brought a visitor to see Denny Ray."

Ellie Peck, the hard-nosed head of the station was thirty years old. She was short and plump with flaming red hair and freckles—and a worthless husband named Mack whom she was mad about. "What's that you've got?" She frowned.

"I brought Bedford to visit Denny Ray."

"That's against the rules."

"Oh, come on, Ellie!" Ket pleaded. "He gets so lonesome in there. And you know there's scientific research that shows it's good to have patients visited by pets."

"That's in a nursing home!"

"Well, if it'll work in a nursing home, it ought to work here. He'll enjoy it so much. Come on. Be a sport."

"Well, I suppose it won't hurt unless you get caught, but if Dr. Bjelland catches you, I'm out of it."

"No problem. I'll take the rap. Thanks, Ellie."

Ket moved down the hall thinking suddenly that she would soon be a fully fledged registered nurse. She had graduated college with a bachelor's degree in science and come to work at Mercy Hospital as a licensed practical nurse, but soon she would be registered and certified and a genuine nurse in every sense of the word. She was eager to complete this certification, but realized that at age twenty-four she was right on track.

Turning into room 417, she glanced quickly at the boy in the bed who was lying flat on his back staring up at the ceiling. Her heart went out to him as it always did. Ten-year-old Denny Ray Kelland was a very appealing boy. He had fine blond hair, light blue eyes, and did not appear to be sick. Ket knew that his heart problem was more severe than Denny Ray guessed, but as always, she greeted him with a bright smile.

"Denny Ray, I brought you a visitor!"

Denny Ray quickly raised his head. When he saw the dog Ket held out, his eyes lit up at once. "Gosh! Is that your dog, Ket?"

"Sure is. His name's Bedford. Here, you'll love him." With this she tossed the Yorkie on the bed. Bedford never met a soul he didn't love or didn't want to lick. Before Denny Ray could put his hands up, the Yorkie had both feet braced against him and was licking him right in the face.

"Hey!" Denny Ray yelled. "You're going to swallow me!"

Ket laughed at the sight. "As you can see, he likes you. Don't let him drown you, though. Let me know if he gets to be too much."

But Denny Ray seemed delighted by the dog's attention. Finally, he grabbed Bedford and held him up. "Gosh, this is a great dog," he said. "What kind is it?"

"He's a Yorkie."

"He's not very big, is he?"

"Not very big! Why, he weighs a thumping seven pounds!" Ket smiled. She came over and sat down on the bed, then reached out and pushed Denny Ray's hair away from his eyes. "You need a haircut. I may do that myself."

"His name is Bedford? Why do you call him that?"

"I named him after one of my heroes, Nathan Bedford Forrest."

"I never heard of him."

"Well, you will when you study the Civil War."

"Was he a Rebel or a Yankee?"

Ket laughed. "Would a Southern girl like me have a Yankee as a hero? No, he was a general in the cavalry. One of the finest in the whole war. I'll bring you a book and read to you about him sometime."

Ket sat beside Denny Ray, watching him play with Bedford. He smiled and laughed more than he had in days, she noticed, but his face was thin and his skin looked almost translucent. *You can almost see that heart wearing him down,* she thought. *Something must be done. Lord, he's too fine a boy for us to lose. Don't let this be the end of him.*

Finally, the nurse on duty came in. Sally O'Brien was one of Ket's best friends, and Sally smiled briefly at Ket before giving Denny Ray and the dog an indulgent look. "My, my. Who let that little guy in?"

"His name is Bedford. He's Ket's dog," Denny Ray said.

"Somehow I had a feeling." Sally walked to the other side of the bed and patted Bedford's head. "Sorry, Denny Ray. I can see you're enjoying your furry visitor, but it's time for your medication and then a bath."

"No, not yet. We're having fun," Denny Ray pleaded.

Ket sighed. It was hard to go, but she didn't want to push her luck breaking hospital rules. "Sally's right. I have to go, Denny Ray." She stood and reached for Bedford, who was frantically stealing a few more licks off the boy's face.

"Will you bring him back sometime?" Denny Ray asked.

"I sure will. When you get out of here, we'll take him to an open field and watch him go. You ought to see Bedford go after a squirrel. He's really something."

"He sure is," Denny Ray agreed, gazing longingly at the dog who now sat alertly at his bedside. "My dad says he's going to get me a dog when I come out of the hospital. Maybe I'll get one like Bedford."

"Maybe." Ket forced a hopeful smile. She hoped with all her heart Denny Ray would be running around with a dog of his own someday.

"Well, got to go. See you tomorrow, pal."

Sally had started checking Denny Ray's blood pressure and looked up at Ket. "Maggie and Debbie went down to the cafeteria for a break," she offered, mentioning their other close friends. "You could probably still catch up with them."

"Thanks, Sally. I think I'll try," Ket said.

Just outside the room, Ket snapped on Bedford's leash and kept him close beside her as they moved down the hall. In order to avoid anyone who might object to Bedford, she took the stairs down to the second floor. As Sally had predicted, she spotted Maggie Stone and Debbie Smith having coffee at a table near the door. Ket plumped herself down in an empty chair.

"Hi. What's going on?"

Maggie stared at her. With short sandy hair and large brown eyes, Maggie was quite attractive. But like so many young women Ket knew, Maggie was always worrying about her weight. Needlessly, too, Ket thought.

"What are you doing here today?"

"I came to see Denny Ray. I thought a visit from Bedford would cheer him up. Can I have a bite of your doughnut?"

She reached out, but Maggie slapped her hand away. "Get your own doughnut." Then she gave Ket a grin. "I shouldn't be breaking my diet, but this is my reward for working a double shift, and I intend to eat every crumb." With that she took a large, tantalizing bite.

"What an adorable dog." Debbie leaned over and

gave Bedford a pat. She and Ket had gone to college together and had felt lucky to find themselves together again at Mercy Hospital. Debbie was sweet and upbeat, with auburn hair and gentle gray eyes. She rarely had a harsh word to say about anybody and had always been a loyal, supportive friend.

"Look. I think he likes me," Debbie said as Bedford tried desperately to climb into her lap.

"He likes everyone," Ket explained. "Here, hold him a minute, will you? I just want to get some coffee." Without waiting for her reply, Ket handed Debbie Bedford's leash and bought herself two doughnuts and a cup of decaf coffee. When she returned to the table, she could tell that Debbie and Maggie were on to their favorite topic again: eligible young men. Or, the lack thereof.

"So, what's going on in your love life, Ket?" Maggie asked. "Anything interesting to report?"

Ket took a huge bite of doughnut and shook her head. "Not too much…but as a matter of fact, I do have a date tonight."

"Who with?" both young women demanded simultaneously.

"I'm not telling. You two are the worst gossips in the hospital. Anyway, I'm not too excited about it."

Debbie said, "I know a fellow that works for the state government. He'd be perfect for you, Ket. Why don't you let me fix you up?"

"I don't think so."

Maggie frowned with disapproval. "You don't need

to miss any chances. A woman who wants a husband has got to—" She broke off suddenly and her eyes widened. The other two were watching her and saw something like shock come over her face. "Who is *that?*" she whispered.

Ket turned casually and then suddenly froze. The sight of the tall man who had just entered the cafeteria with Dr. Lars Bjelland had an almost paralyzing effect on her.

"Now, he is *something!*" Debbie breathed. "Did you ever see a better-looking man in your whole life?"

The man that Debbie and Maggie were staring at was six foot five, with a lean, athletic-looking build. He had auburn hair, light blue eyes and strong, even features. Both Maggie and Debbie watched with shock as he suddenly turned toward them and smiled. "He's coming over here," Debbie said.

"Do you know him?" Maggie whispered.

Ket had no time to answer for the tall man stopped before them and looked down at her. "Hello, Ket," he said.

"Hello, Jared. It's nice to see you."

"You're a nurse here?"

"I'm almost through with my training."

"Mom said she got a letter from your mother telling her you were almost done." His warm smile made him even more attractive. "I guess we'll be seeing each other from time to time. I'm going to intern here at Mercy." Then he glanced across the room and said, "Dr. Bjelland's waiting. Good to see you."

The three young women watched in stunned silence as he walked away. "Who is that?" Maggie finally gasped.

"Jared Pierce."

"And you know him?" Debbie breathed. "Tell us *all* about it!"

"Oh, we grew up together. Went to the same school."

"What a cutie!" Debbie sighed. "Did you date him?"

"No," Ket said shortly. "He was a couple of grades above me—and besides, we didn't get along."

"Didn't get along with a guy like that?" Maggie snorted. "You were out of your mind!"

"Don't be fooled by appearances, ladies," Ket warned. "When I think of Jared Pierce, all I can remember is a rather nasty boy who teased me about being so tall. He was always puling my ponytail, and once he pushed me into a mud puddle."

"He could push me into the Atlantic Ocean!" Debbie grinned.

"Well, he was the star of the baseball team. All the girls were chasing him." Ket shrugged. "He wouldn't have looked at me if my hair was on fire."

They all three watched as the two doctors got their trays and made their way to a table.

"Look at that," Maggie said. "Every woman in here has her eyes on that man. Ket, you've got to introduce me to him."

"It wouldn't do you any good. He's like all stars, pretty stuck-up."

"Maybe he's changed," Debbie said. "He came over and spoke to you right away."

"And that's probably the last time he'll speak to me unless he needs my help around here in the medical line for some reason. Which is doubtful." Ket suddenly lost her appetite. "Here, you can have my other doughnut." She passed a doughnut to Maggie, then reached down and handed the last morsel of one she had almost finished to Bedford. "Come on, Bedford. We've got to get home."

"Hey, I want to hear all about that date tomorrow!" Maggie called out but Ket did not even turn around.

Out in the parking lot, Ket got into the car and plunked Bedford down on the seat beside her. She started the engine and drove home, her mind on Jared Pierce. Her mother had once been best friends with Jared's mother, but the Pierce family had moved away years ago, so their friendship had been sustained by phone calls and letters.

"Jared Pierce," she mused. "Well, he's something, I have to admit. As mean and stuck-up as he was, I would definitely have dated him if he'd just given me a look, but he never did."

Arriving at the house she went quickly inside, unsnapped Bedford's leash. "Go get something to eat," she said, and watched the dog scurry off.

Turning, she went into the den where she found her mother ironing and watching television. Her mother was a news hound and spent most of her time watching the all-news TV channels.

"Why, Ket, you're home early. Did you see your young friend?"

"Yes, I did."

"How was he?"

"Not good. He's so sick and he doesn't really know it."

"I bet he enjoyed Bedford, though."

"Yes, he did. He's so sweet. He enjoys everything you do for him and is so appreciative."

Flinging herself onto the recliner, Ket sat watching her mother for a time. With dark auburn hair, warm dark eyes and a trim figure, Lucille Lindsey was still an attractive woman at age forty-eight. Ketura thought she had to be the most devoted wife and mother in the world…at least in all of Texas. Now that Ket was an adult, she could appreciate how hard her mother had worked raising her three children—Ket and her two older sisters, Carol and Jenny. Though they'd squabbled and teased each other almost constantly while growing up, Ketura missed her sisters and wished she could see them more often. Carol, an elementary school teacher, had recently married and lived in Southern California, where her husband worked for a computer software firm. Jenny was in Chicago, finishing law school. She and her boyfriend had announced their engagement the past Christmas and would be married next year. Ketura was happy for them, but wasn't looking forward to the event. She felt embarrassed to be the only sister left who was unmarried—and with absolutely no prospects in sight. She dreaded the well-meaning questions and romantic advice of relatives and family friends she'd surely hear on her sister's wedding day. Ketura hoped to be far away by then, doing missionary work in India, which was her plan once she'd completed her training and became a registered nurse.

While her parents were proud that she had been called to such an admirable vocation, Ketura knew that they were anxious about her going so far away on her own. Mostly, her parents wanted to see her "settled down with a nice young man"—just like her sisters. She knew her mother worried the most, but her mom was quieter about it than her father. While she and her sisters had been growing up, Ket knew she'd always been the most mischievous, and her mother deserved a medal for her patience.

And I'm still testing her patience, Ket thought, casting her mother an affectionate glance.

Ket sighed. She popped the chair back into the reclining position and watched the news for a time but was not really interested. "Guess who I saw today, Mom?" she asked suddenly.

"Who?"

"Jared Pierce."

This did catch Lucille Lindsey's attention. "Did you really! Where in the world did you see him?"

"In the hospital. He's come to do his internship there."

"I knew he was an intern now. Irene told me. But I didn't know it would be in your hospital. Did you talk to him at all?" she asked eagerly.

"Oh, he came over and said hello."

"And what did you say?"

"I said, 'Hello, Jared.'"

"Is that all?" Lucille was plainly disappointed. "After all, you're old schoolmates."

"Not really. He was in the twelfth grade when I was in the tenth. That's like two different species. He was about as interested in me as he was in the carvings on Mount Rushmore."

"Oh, don't be silly! You and Jared played together all your lives."

Ket did not answer for a time, then she said, "Well, I will say he's still fine looking. So tall. I thought Maggie and Debbie were going to faint when they saw him."

"Well, he's dating someone. Irene told me that. Oh, you'd know her!"

"How would I know her?"

"Why, she's one of your old schoolmates. Lisa Glenn."

"He's dating Lisa?"

"Yes. You know she's Miss Texas now."

"I knew that. She was always Miss Something. Miss Mudpie or Miss Ingrown Toenail."

"Now, that's not kind! She's a pretty girl, and she just naturally likes beauty contests."

"I know, Mom. I just never got along with Lisa very well. I always thought she was *pretty* stuck-up."

Her mother missed the pun, Ket noticed, but Ket didn't bother explaining it.

"Well, I suppose she may have been but, in any case, she and Jared are dating."

"Are they engaged?"

"No. Not yet. Irene said she's hoping they will be. She's very fond of Lisa."

Suddenly Ket came to her feet. "Here. Let me finish that ironing. Most of it's mine anyway." She ignored her mother's protests and picked up the iron. Lucille gathered up a pile of neatly folded clothing. "Don't forget. You've got a date tonight," she reminded Ket as she left the room.

"I know it," Ket said shortly. She almost added, "And do I dread it," but she did not. Her parents were always excited when she went out with someone. Both of them longed to see her find a nice boyfriend but Ket felt as if she was constantly disappointing them.

"Well, it's a date anyhow, and that's more than I've had lately," she told herself as she pressed down viciously on the blouse and then suddenly lifted the iron. "No sense taking it out on you." She thought of Jared Pierce then, and murmured, "Hmph. He was a real pest when he was a kid, and I expect he's about the same deep down. Lisa is welcome to him!"

Chapter Two

"Well, at least I'm not *quite* six feet tall—guess I should be grateful. Another quarter of an inch I would be."

Why couldn't I have been petite and beautiful like Carol and Jenny instead of tall and plain? Ever since she could remember, Ket had longed to look like her two older sisters. Both of them had taken their size and beauty from their mother—exactly five foot four with dark auburn hair and sparkling, dark eyes. Both of them had attracted more suitors than Quaker has oats. Ketura had a sharp memory of the time when she was an adolescent, coming into her full growth and her father had admonished her sharply. "Ketura, for goodness' sake, will you straighten up! You look like Quasimodo!"

Ket had finally been cured of stooping over to minimize her height by recognizing that it did not help.

Also by realizing that God, in His infinite wisdom, had chosen to make her different from her mother and sisters. Different from most women, in fact. She knew by now there was no use complaining about it.

Now she stood straight and tall and put her attention fully on the dress that she had bought for tonight. At one time in her life she had envisioned herself going out for dates as often as her sisters, but somehow her shyness with men—mostly because of her height—had brought her to a strange situation in which she had almost stopped dating completely. She refused to date anyone shorter than she was, which eliminated fifty percent of the male population, and the other fifty percent were put off by what they considered her haughty manner. She was not haughty actually, but hid her real feelings. She feared rejection and did all she could to avoid embarrassment and humiliation.

She examined the dress critically, for she had bought it especially for her date with Charlie Petrie. Petrie was not handsome, but he was six feet three inches tall. True enough, he was thin, almost to the point of disappearing if he stood sideways. His colleagues at the accounting firm where he worked called him Ichabod behind his back, for his stooped, thin frame reminded one of the character in the classic by Washington Irving.

"This stupid dress makes me look awful!" Staring at herself, Ketura turned around and studied it. She had paid more for it than she had ever thought she would spend for a dress. Indeed, her trip to Neiman Marcus in Dallas had been her first. She had felt like a poor relation and was certain she had seen disdain in the eyes of the cool-voiced saleswoman who had waited on her.

As she recalled how embarrassing the trip to Neiman Marcus had been, Ketura flushed. She did have one outstanding trait, and that was her beautiful complexion. It was as smooth and clear as a woman's skin could be, but she never saw that quality and remained distracted by the few faint freckles across the bridge of her nose that she considered unsightly. Now she looked again at the dress and tried to find something good about it. She had not liked it much at the store, but the saleswoman had talked her into buying it. "With your height, you have to wear a style like this, dear," the woman had said.

"Like what?" Ketura wondered aloud now. "Like somebody's spinster aunt?"

That's who the dress seemed suited for, she thought, despairing as she studied her reflection. The short-sleeved button-front chemise, made from a smooth, pale yellow fabric, fell just below her knees. The demure oval neckline was outlined with satin appliqué, and the tiny buttons covered in satin, as well.

Maybe it wasn't that bad, she decided, but so out of sync with her usual, sporty style that she felt as though she were dressed in a costume.

Ketura finally turned and sat down at the edge of her bed to put on her shoes. The shoes were also new and rather attractive, and Ketura had surprisingly small feet for her height. The shoes were overpriced though, and now she wished she'd put her hard-earned money toward something more practical, like a good pair of jogging shoes. Or better yet, used the money for a donation to people who had no shoes at all.

While slipping them on, she glanced at the clock on her bedside table. "Time for Cinderella to go to the ball," she muttered darkly.

She went downstairs and found her parents in the family room. Her father greeted her with a smile. "Well, now," he said with appreciation, "don't you look nice, Ket."

He came over to stand beside her, and no one seeing them together could mistake their relationship. Roger Lindsey was six foot three with blue eyes and blond hair that had gone mostly gray. For a man of fifty, few lines marked his face or marred his strong features. Ketura always felt she was looking at a masculine version of herself when she looked into her father's face.

"I hate this dress," she murmured between clenched teeth.

"Hate it? Why, how can you say that?" Her mother looked genuinely surprised. "You look lovely. I'm sure Charlie will think so, too."

"I paid too much for the dress and the shoes. Just think what the mission in Bombay could have done with that money."

"Well, that's very true," her mother replied placidly. "But young women need new clothes once in a while,

too, and you told me yourself that you didn't have anything to wear for tonight."

Roger looked at his wife and shook his head. "I
have to agree with Ketura. I remember it was Thoreau
who said, 'Beware of all enterprises that require new
clothes.'" He smiled and his eyes crinkled up at the cor-
ners. "Besides, Charlie probably won't know the difference. I don't think he appreciates anything but
numbers."

The skinny, dull accountant wasn't the man for his
Ket, Roger thought. Still, it was good to see her going
out tonight and having some fun. He studied his daughter, who now sat on the couch next to his wife, and
couldn't help but wonder why she had not been as popular and sought-after as her older sisters. They had gone
through dozens of boyfriends during high school and
college, and Roger remembered finding the house
crowded with them—gawky young men—everywhere
you turned. This had not been the case with Ket, and it
hurt him somehow, for he knew that this younger
daughter of his who looked so much like him felt inse-
cure. He had wanted to say, *Don't compare yourself to
your sisters, Ket. They are who they are and you're
what God made you. A tall, strong, beautiful woman in
your own right.*

However, he had never been able to find an opportunity to say this. So now he said, "I think you look beautiful, sweetheart."

"Thank you, Daddy." Ketura smiled, despite herself.
It was just her dad and she knew he felt obliged to say

such things, but the compliment made her feel good nonetheless.

"It's about time for Charlie to get here, isn't it? Where are you going?" he asked.

"We're going to the movies. Some film about space travel. Scientists are stranded on another planet. Or maybe they get stranded on the *way* to another planet.... I'm not quite sure."

Her mother glanced at her with a puzzled expression. "I thought you hated movies like that."

"Well...it wasn't my first choice. But Charlie thought it would be fun."

Ketura shrugged and forced a smile. She actually dreaded a two-hour simulated ride through outer space, which would either put her to sleep, or give her a whopper of a headache with the earsplitting special effects. But, while pretending to give her some say in the matter, Charlie had pushed his preference. She'd sensed that if she didn't give in and agree, he'd most likely sit pouting through any film that was her choice.

Her father returned to the book he'd been reading and Ket watched a news show with her mother. Seven-thirty came and still no Charlie Petrie. Ket felt partly relieved, partly annoyed and partly anxious, anticipating she might be stood up. Finally, at seven-forty-five the phone rang.

"I'll get it," Lucille said. She went over, picked up the phone and said, "Hello? Oh, yes, she's right here. Tell her *what?*" She hung up the phone and turned slowly to face Ket, a worried frown on her face.

Suddenly Ket knew what had brought the frown to her mother's face. She stood and said quietly, "He's not coming, is he?"

Lucille Lindsey shot an agonized glance at her husband and then turned back to face Ket. "No, he said something had come up—an emergency of some kind."

Ket met her mother's sympathetic gaze for a moment and felt her eyes fill with tears. She took a deep breath and willed herself not to cry.

"Right. An accounting emergency. Someone forgot to file their taxes. They just realized it," she joked. Her parents both smiled but neither laughed, she noticed.

Ket avoided looking at them. She sat very still and stared straight ahead. She felt something happening deep within, in some silent, invincible place.

She suddenly became aware that a resolution was forming inside, while not in words, in some way she was saying, *I won't be put through this kind of humiliation again!* With an effort she kept her face straight and shrugged. "Well, all dressed up and no place to go."

"Let the three of us go see a movie. I wouldn't mind getting out tonight," Roger said quickly. He saw the pain that had flickered across his daughter's face and wanted to do something to take it away. He knew that her pride had been hurt badly, and anger washed through him. *I'd like to tell that Charlie Petrie what I think of him! To treat a young woman like this…!* However, he could say none of this, for a look from his wife, who knew him very well, stilled him on that subject.

"Oh, I don't think so, Daddy. Why don't you and

Mom go? I think I'll just change clothes and go out for a little drive."

Watching as Ket walked stiffly out of the room, her parents waited until the sound of her footsteps faded.

"Oh, Roger, I'm so worried about Ket! She's not happy."

"I know she isn't, but I don't know what to do about it." His glance moved to the portraits of their three daughters on the mantle over the fireplace. He studied them for a moment and shook his head. "She's always putting herself down. She doesn't think she's as pretty as Carol or Jenny."

"I know, and that's wrong. Carol and Jenny have a different kind of beauty."

"Well, that's true enough. They look like you. I wish Ket had taken after you instead of me."

"Don't say that, Roger!" Lucille came over and put her arm around her husband. "God made her just as she is."

"I know. I wanted to tell her that, but somehow I never can."

Shaking her head almost in despair, Lucille said quietly, "It's something she'll have to come to on her own. It's strange, Roger. She's such a fine girl. So honest and strong in every way. So bright and caring."

"And such a clear thinker, too! She can read other people, but she's never really figured herself out."

Upstairs, Ketura pulled off the dress and tossed it across the room where it landed on the floor in a heap. Such anger was rare for her, but Charlie Petrie's rejection had stung terribly. She didn't know why it hurt so much. She didn't even really like him and didn't respect him anymore, either. He was such a coward. He didn't even have the nerve to cancel on her himself, but had left her mother to do it. Who needed a guy like that?

Picking up her dress and throwing it across a chair, she yanked off the shoes and panty hose, then pulled on a pair of comfortable khakis, a favorite blue polo shirt, socks and sneakers. Feeling much better, she grabbed her purse and left the house. She got into her blue convertible, started the engine and put the top down. She'd bought the car used, at a reasonable price, but it was still the most impulsive, frivolous purchase of her life. The aging vehicle wasn't even entirely reliable, but Ket loved the feeling of freedom she experienced while driving with the top down. The wind ruffled her hair as she pulled away from the house and cruised down the street, and Ket felt all her cares blown away with it.

Fragments of the sunset threw a magenta haze over the west for the summer had brought the long days. Now she drove without thinking, just anxious to get away. Swerving and changing lanes, Ket thought of how her life had been so successful in some ways and such a failure in others. Scholastically, she had always excelled and now in her last months of training for her R.N. she was known at Mercy Hospital as an excellent new nurse. She had always been successful at sports, too, and one tennis pro had told her she could make a living at the game, if she wanted to give her life to it. Ketura had laughed at him. "Tennis isn't something you give your life to. I need more than that."

She reached the interstate and as soon as she was clear of the Dallas city traffic, she stepped on the accelerator. As always, as the wind rushed toward her and the road swept by, she experienced that delight in the open car that she could not explain.

She drove for nearly an hour, enjoying her solitude, then finally turned back toward the city. As she sent the car through the darkness, she listened to her favorite station on the radio. It was typical that she would listen to such a station, which played the nostalgia music of the forties and fifties—the famous big bands and the great vocalists of that era. Somehow the music soothed her, and when she got back to Dallas she turned off the highway abruptly and soon found herself at a place she knew very well—the parking lot of the ballpark in Arlington—home field of her favorite major league team.

She parked the convertible, got out and began to walk. There was no ball game that night. The team was on a road trip. The skies had turned a velvety blue-black hue now, and overhead a Cheshire cat moon grinned down at her. The stars were sprinkled liberally overhead, and the air of night felt warm. She moved toward the stadium itself, the home plate entrance, and when she got there thought how different it was here when there was no game. The sound of traffic—of heavy trucks and smaller cars—came to her like a distant hum not unlike that of bees. But here there was a quietness that was almost palpable. Looking up, she walked up to the barred gates and wished that there were a game tonight to take her mind off her ruined evening. She loved baseball and could quote innumerable statistics to the amusement of her father and the displeasure of her mother. "It's not ladylike," Lucille always said with a frown. But something about the game—ribald and rough as it was—pleased her.

Finally she turned and began walking over the vacant parking lot, acres and acres of concrete with the tall poles bearing light all around. As she walked her mind returned again and again to the debacle of her date with Charlie Petrie. "I don't even *like* him," she announced aloud, her voice breaking the silence. And she continued to speak aloud as she sometimes did when she was in places where she was absolutely certain no one could hear. "He has absolutely nothing that would appeal to me. He doesn't care anything at all about the things that I like. He wouldn't even go to church with me. That's enough for me to turn him down, but I didn't! I agreed to go see that stupid movie with him! Why did I do it?"

Abruptly she turned away as if trying to turn away from her own thoughts, but they followed her as she circled one of the huge light poles and meandered around the acres of empty parking lot. But as she did, she faced the truth about herself. "I wanted a date. I wanted some man to like me. What's wrong with that? Every woman likes that!"

The argument seemed sound enough, but somehow

Ket was not happy with it. She turned, shaking her head, and moved back to her car. Instead of getting in, she leaned against it, fixed her eyes on the stadium, thought of the lights and the cheers and the screams of the crowd when one of her favorite players knocked the ball out of the park, and wished again that there were a game. Finally, however, she opened the door and got in. Settling behind the wheel, she said, "I guess I've got to face up to it." She gripped the steering wheel hard until her hands ached, then spoke up firmly, "I'm never going to find a Prince Charming. There'll be no wedding bells or family for me. I'll have to fill my life up with other things!"

Overhead she saw the Cheshire cat moon grinning—old silver glowing in the sky—but it gave her no pleasure. Still speaking aloud softly, she argued with herself. "I really should count my blessings. I have so much. I've got a good family. I've got a good church—and I've found a career I love. A lot of women would like to have all of that. And I have India."

The thought of India washed over her quickly—images of Bombay where she had already made two mission trips with a team of doctors and nurses. Her heart had been touched by that place and the terrible conditions of the people there. She remembered a tiny woman that she had found in the streets, emaciated and drawn, and somehow the love of God had flowed through her and she had sat down and held the woman until she died in her arms. From that moment she had known that someday she would serve God as a medical missionary in India.

"Yes, I've got India. That's my future. Something to work toward. My life can really make a difference. As for Prince Charming, who needs him? Even if I met a man I really liked, that would only complicate things. God obviously doesn't want me to get involved with anyone right now, so I'll be free to do the work He's called me to," she reasoned.

With determination she started up the car and headed toward the exit. Somehow she knew that this night had changed her life. "No Prince Charming for me," she murmured as she headed toward home.

When she reached the house, Ket was surprised to see that the lights were still on. She went inside and found her father, dressed in his pajamas and a robe, sitting at the kitchen table. He was dipping graham crackers into a glass of milk—his favorite snack. Looking up, he said at once, "I've been worried about you, Ket."

"Oh, I'm all right. You shouldn't have waited up."

Roger Lindsey sat there struggling for words. The love he had for this daughter of his was enormous. Perhaps it was because she needed him more than his other two daughters, although he cared deeply for them. Now he dipped a graham cracker into the milk, bit it off, swallowed then said, "Try not to care too much. He's not worth it."

"No, he's not." Forcing a smile, Ket came over and put her arm around her father. "Don't worry about me, Dad. I'm all right. I have plenty going on in my life. I have plans. My training will be over soon, and I'll be an R.N."

"And then you'll be going off to India and leaving us."

"Yes, but that's what God has called me to do. So, you wouldn't want me to do anything else, would you?"

"No, I wouldn't." He stood, suddenly put his arms around Ket and hugged her tightly. "I'm very proud of you, daughter," he said huskily. Then he turned and left the room, saying, "I'll see you tomorrow."

Ket quickly showered, put on her nightgown, but she was thinking of her father. *He wants to help,* she thought, *but he doesn't know how a woman who's rejected feels. I don't think any man could ever understand that—but he's a sweet thing. Why can't I find one like him, who loves tall plain girls?*

Finally she got into bed, turned the reading light on and propped herself up. Picking up the thick Bible from her bedside table, she began to read. The Bible was her favorite book. She read other things, of course, but this was the one that really appealed to her. She was reading now all the way through the Bible from Genesis to Revelation and had reached the thirtieth chapter of Isaiah. He was her favorite among the major prophets, and she settled down, forcibly putting everything out of her mind except the text that was before her. She had an enviable way of focusing on the thing at hand. Other things might occur, but once she was in this mode, whether it was studying medicine or the Bible, or reading a poem, she had learned the secret of total concentration.

She began reading and the first verse said, "Woe to the rebellious children, saith the Lord, that take counsel, but not of Me." She thought about that for a moment, for she also had the habit of reading a verse, stopping and thinking, and meditating upon it. "A hard thing to say to the old Israelites," she murmured. Then she read the second verse, which said, "That walk to go down into Egypt, and have not asked at My mouth; to strengthen themselves in the strength of Pharaoh, and to trust in the shadows of Egypt!"

Somehow the verse seemed to reach out. "This is really a tough thing. God is saying that the old Hebrews trusted the strength of Pharaoh rather than putting their trust in the Lord God."

And as always, she tried to make a personal application. *Lord, have I done that? Have I trusted in something else beside You? You know I don't want to do that, for You are my hope and my trust. And I love You more than anyone else, or anything else. So, let me trust You and not in Egypt or anything this world offers me.*

A sense of approval and peacefulness came to her. It was not something she could have described to anyone else, but as she prayed and meditated, Ket often felt that when she surrendered herself to God, He gave His approval by this sort of feeling. Suddenly a startling thought touched her. *Maybe I've been trusting the worldly things to get a husband instead of trusting God.*

The thought disturbed her for it was almost as if a hand had been laid on her. Slowly she began to review her life. She was well aware that all women did things to make themselves attractive and, deny it as they might, they laid plans to get a husband. It was not a thing women talked about, for traditionally the man was the one expected to do the pursuing. Women did not bait traps and catch husbands that way—at least none of them that she had known admitted it.

She sat there for a long time. The only sound was the antique clock that had belonged to her grandparents slowly beating out the time. It made a solitary echo in her room as she thought, *It's not wrong for a woman to dress up and to make herself attractive, is it, Lord?* She didn't seem to get an answer, but somehow an uneasiness filled her. She continued to read and then finally in the fifteenth verse, one of those moments came when the verse seemed to jump off the page. It was almost as if it leapt right into her heart, it struck with such force.

"For thus saith the Lord God, the Holy One of Israel; In returning and rest shall ye be saved; in quietness and in confidence shall be your strength...."

Somehow the verse nudged at Ket, and she paused again and thought, *"In quietness and confidence shall be your strength." Well, I haven't done that. I remember back when I was just fifteen how I tried to be like Carol and Jenny and the other girls. I tried everything in the book to catch a boyfriend, but somehow I never was able.*

She thought again of the embarrassments and the humiliation she had endured to make herself popular, and how those attempts had failed. Oh, she had attracted a few, but no one that had pleased her. Now she went back and studied the words again.

Lord, are You telling me to just be quiet in returning and rest shall ye be saved? To just let You have this thing?

Again she waited, listening for the impression of some kind to come from God. She had never heard the voice of God literally and did not expect to. Still, there had been so many times in her life when after a long prayer, and sometimes even fasting, God had "spoken" so clearly within her spirit that she knew that God was speaking to her in this way. Now she waited, and the longer she waited the more strongly she believed that the verse was speaking directly to her heart. *All right. I'll rest and wait on You. You'll be my strength, Lord.*

She was growing sleepy now but she continued to read, and when she got to the twentieth verse, once again she was brought up short. "And though the Lord give you the bread of adversity, and the water of affliction, yet shall not thy teachers be removed into a corner any more, but thine eyes shall see thy teachers."

She thought, *What does that mean, Lord?* and then the first part of the verse came to her, and she thought, *"The bread of adversity and the water of affliction." I guess that's what I've had as far as romance is concerned. I haven't had any victory there.*

She looked down then and read aloud the twenty-first verse. "'And thine ears shall hear a Word behind thee, saying, This is the way, walk ye in it, when ye turn to the right hand, and when ye turn to the left.'"

At that moment Ketura *knew* that God was giving her a promise. It happened before, more than once, and she felt a sudden glad joy as she realized that this was God's way of speaking to her. *I'm going to hear a voice that will tell me what to do. Is that right, Lord?* She was very sleepy and closed the Bible. Turning out the light, she lay back and began to repeat the twenty-first verse over and over again. "'And thine ears shall hear a Word behind thee, saying, This is the way.'" *Lord, that's what I want,* she prayed silently.

Sleep came but she did not sleep well. More than once she almost came out of her sleep, and finally when dawn came she awakened.

As soon as consciousness came to her, she had one of those mystic moments when she knew that she was in the presence of the Lord. And the Lord was saying in her heart and in her spirit, and in her mind: *This is the way, walk ye in it. Obey me and I will give you a husband....*

Ket's eyes flew open and she gasped. "Give me a husband! Surely that's not what God's saying to me!" But she lay there pleading to God for a long time, and the impression did not cease.

Finally Ketura took a deep breath. *All right, God. If I'm going to have a husband, You'll have to give him to me because I'm not hunting for Prince Charming on my own anymore!*

Chapter Three

Ketura laid her pen down and flexed the fingers of her right hand. They were aching from writing steadily in her diary for the past hour. Now as she leaned back and studied what she had written, a wry thought came to her. *Here I am like a teenage girl, keeping a journal. How sophomoric!*

Perhaps it was unusual for someone to keep a journal faithfully for so many years, but it had become a part of Ket's life. The first page went all the way back to when she was seven years old and had announced firmly to her mother, "I'm going to keep a diary all my life." Her mother had smiled indulgently, but Ket had found putting her thoughts and emotions on paper a good way to analyze who she was. The shelf in her closet now was filled with a line of blank books bought at the bookstore, all of them filled. From time to time she took them out and studied the careful, adolescent handwriting of her early years, finding that almost as interesting as the contents. It had amused her at times to see how earthshaking and traumatic certain events were to a fourteen-year-old, such as making an error in a softball game, which had cost the team the championship. She had written plainly "I think I'll kill myself!" at the end of that entry.

Now, however, her life as it was capsuled onto these pages had become more important to her. Ever since she had started feeling like a giantess, as she put it, and lacked the prettiness that attracted boys, she had recorded her feelings on the pages instead of sharing them with someone else.

Now as she half closed her eyes and thought how horrified she would be if anyone were to read her journals, the impulse came to burn them all. It was not the first time she had thought of such a thing, but she knew she could not do that for these books had become like old friends to her.

Maybe one day when I'm an old, old woman I'll read these, and what I'm thinking will seem as foolish as my actions do at the present. She leaned forward, straightened, arched her back and read what she had written.

April 6

I hardly know how to put down what I feel. I have always been so resistant and even had superior feelings for those who said, "God told me to do such and such." It always seemed to me that they were boasting that they had a straight line to God that the rest of us lacked. I still feel that way— but for the past three days I have been haunted by what has happened.

Does God really speak to people in dreams and in visions? Oh, I know He did speak in such a way to characters in the Bible, but surely now we have the Bible. And why would He speak to me? It would seem likely that if He spoke to anyone so directly, it would be to His chosen vessels—missionaries on the field, evangelists, people working in hard situations in the inner city. Those people whom I admire so much need a direct voice from God.

I can't get away from it! I heard nothing that could have been caught on a tape recorder or was an audible voice, and yet still within my mind, or heart, or soul—or wherever it is that that part of us who talks and listens to God resides—it keeps coming back over and over again, "and thine ears shall hear a Word behind thee saying, This is the way, walk ye in it."

Oh, Lord, I am ready to listen to any Word You have to say—but what Word! Are You really saying that You're going to bring a man into my life who will be my husband? My head is full of strange, confused thoughts, and I haven't been able to work as I should for the past three days. People are starting to give me strange looks, but still that verse keeps coming into my heart. Is it from You, or is it what a psychiatrist would call wish fulfillment? I have no idea, but, Lord, if it's not from You, I pray this morning that You would take it completely out of my mind!

Quickly she put the top on her pen, closed the diary and put it in the drawer beneath her underthings. She wondered if the diary was safe there from prying eyes, and the ridiculous notion came, *Well, what if I got killed? They would find it and read it.*

Giving a short laugh, she rose and said, "I wouldn't care then. I'd be in heaven. Maybe they'd get a good laugh out of it."

Going downstairs, she ate a quick breakfast, then left at once for the hospital. She had learned to handle the Dallas traffic, and taking every shortcut and weaving in and out she arrived with fifteen minutes to spare. Getting out of the car, she looked up at the massive, white marble with which Mercy Hospital was built. Appreciating once again the fact that she had had a good year, her first year as an L.P.N.—licensed, practical nurse. She remembered how frightened she had been when she had come there for the first time.

Entering briskly, she went at once to the third floor and found Maggie Stone waiting for her, her brown eyes were snapping and her sandy hair escaped out from under her white cap. "You'd better watch out for Dr. Bjelland. He's on the war path today!"

Fastening her cap more securely, Ket took a deep breath. "What's it about this time?"

"I don't know. Does he need a reason?" Maggie was one year older than Ket and wanted two things in this world, and she kept neither of them a secret. First she wanted to finish her nursing degree. Second, she wanted a husband, a goal she would announce straightforwardly to anyone. "Not a doctor. A stockbroker perhaps," she'd specify. "Someone who doesn't bring any problems home with him." Why Maggie should have thought stockbrokers had no problems, Ket could not imagine. But now as the two left the dressing room and went down the halls, she listened as Maggie explained why the man she had been dating definitely would not do.

The two young women were caught up at once in the busy life of a huge hospital. Ket was assigned to the cardiac ward, a duty that affected her more profoundly than she had ever known. It was worse to her than the emergency room. There the cases often entered in critical conditions sometimes, with patients dying and always frightened. That was difficult, of course—but in the cardiac ward there was an ominous air that seemed to permeate even the furniture and the walls. Fear was a part of the atmosphere that all patients shared, and as Ket went about her duties she made it a point to spend as much time with those who were most anxious and apprehensive.

It was midway through the morning when Ket spotted the interns following Dr. Lars Bjelland as he entered her unit on his rounds. Bjelland was a Norwegian with a trace of his roots in his speech. Rotund with a square face and a shock of iron-gray hair, at the age of fifty-five he looked more like a plumber than a skilled surgeon. His eyes were pale blue and he had the huge hands of a farmer. He attacked medicine the way that his ancestors probably attacked a Saxon village: with all his strength and dragging everyone along with him.

While Ket found Dr. Bjelland abrasive, she knew he was a good doctor and she admired his skill and experience. Still, she was not in the mood for one of his confrontations today and tried her best to avoid him and the flock of interns that followed in his wake. Just like every other woman on the unit, she couldn't help but notice Jared Pierce among the group, standing a head taller than the others and twice as handsome. While some of the nurses seemed determined to throw themselves in the path of the roaming herd, Jared's presence was another reason for Ketura to sidestep them.

But to her dismay, she was looking in on Denny Ray when the entire group filed into the room. Ketura felt like a salmon, swimming against the stream as she tried to quietly make her way to the door. With her gaze down, she slowly worked her way toward the exit, weaving her way around the interns while, across the room, Dr. Bjelland lectured.

"Excuse me…excuse me…" she mumbled, working her way through the crowd. Ketura had almost reached freedom when suddenly she collided with something— or someone. She stumbled for a second, then a strong grip seized her shoulders and helped her regain her balance.

"Ketura—sorry. I didn't see you there," a deep voice apologized.

Her gaze flew up and met Jared Pierce's surprised expression. She stared into his blue eyes for a second and then quickly stepped back, bumping into a plastic chair.

"My fault," she mumbled.

The incident took only seconds, but still attracted Dr. Bjelland's attention. He paused in his lesson and pinned Ketura with a steely glance.

"You there. Nurse Lindsey. Stop the chatter please. You can learn from this conversation, too. It wouldn't hurt, you know."

"Yes, Doctor. Please go on. Sorry for the interruption." Ketura turned and faced Dr. Bjelland, giving her full attention now like the interns. She knew she was trapped, unable to leave until Bjelland dismissed them. She stood wedged between Jared and the plastic chair, shoulder to shoulder with him, but trying her best to ignore his unnerving proximity.

Of course he didn't see me. Nearly six feet tall, but no matter. I've always been invisible to Jared Pierce. Ket glanced at the tall, handsome man beside her and the impression was once again confirmed. He seemed no more aware of her than he was of the furniture. His attention was completely focused on Dr. Bjelland as the senior physician talked on about Denny Ray's symptoms and condition, medical information Ketura knew by heart by now.

Her mind strayed and she thought again of the verse

that had come to her, going endlessly over the question in her mind. *Is this feeling, this message truly from God?* Then a second question would soon follow. *If God's going to send me a husband, how will He do it, and how will I know him? What will he be like?*

Suddenly there was a silence. Ket blinked and came out of her reverie. She felt everyone staring at her, including Jared Pierce and her favorite patient, Denny Ray Kelland. She turned her gaze to Dr. Bjelland and knew at once that he had spoken to her and she had missed it completely.

"I—I'm sorry, Dr. Bjelland, I didn't hear you."

"Do you have a hearing problem, Nurse Lindsey?"

"No, sir."

"You didn't hear me, but you don't have a hearing problem? How do you account for that?"

"I suppose…that I let my mind drift for a minute."

"Well, that's fine! I invited you to participate in a learning opportunity with these doctors and perhaps share your special knowledge of this young patient with us—and you have let your mind drift! What were you thinking of? Share it with us. It must be very important for you to leave all care of your patient to indulge yourself in it."

Ket swallowed. She felt her cheeks flush. She'd always been a favorite of Dr. Bjelland, but she was now discovering how it felt when the keen blade of his sarcasm slashed out. She had seen others demolished, cut off at the knees practically, when this had happened, but she had never found herself under the knife.

"I'm sorry," she said quietly. "It won't happen again, Dr. Bjelland."

"I should hope not!" Bjelland glared at her for a moment, and for a moment she was afraid he was about to deliver another harsh word. But instead, she nearly jumped out of her skin when she felt Jared's gentle touch on her arm; it lasted but a moment, just long enough to signal his silent support.

"I'm not sure I heard your question that clearly, either, Dr. Bjelland." Jared's voice was confident and steady, despite the senior doctor's intimidating manner that had the other interns shaking in their boots. "There were some orderlies passing with a cleaning cart. It was quite noisy on this end of the room."

Dr. Bjelland cast him a doubtful look, but Ket noticed that Jared's gaze did not waver. She'd been so lost in thought herself, she honestly couldn't say now if a cleaning cart had passed or not.

"A cleaning cart, eh?" Dr. Bjelland shook his head. He wouldn't give in so easily. Not to an intern. "I thought she was perhaps considering what color of lipstick she might wear on her date tonight."

"She don't date," Denny Ray countered.

The exchange drew a burst of nervous laughter from the group. All except Jared, Ket noticed. She felt her cheeks glow even redder, though she didn't think it possible. She knew Dr. Bjelland was looking at her again, but didn't dare meet his gaze.

"She doesn't date? Well, that's good. The rest of the young women around her are all chasing men full-time. This hospital is just a happy hunting ground for them."

Ketura hoped the discussion of her social life would end there, but she wasn't going to be that fortunate, she realized. Bjelland looked back at the boy saying, "So, she doesn't date. How do you know?"

"She told me."

"I see. Well, you two must be pretty close friends for her to speak so intimately to you. Is that right?"

"Sure, she comes to see me all the time when she's off-duty."

Dr. Bjelland turned his head and did not speak for a moment. Ket, however, knew him well and saw the approval in his steady eyes, but he only said, "Very commendable. Well, I guess that's all for you this morning. Maybe I'll come back and visit you myself on my off time. Will that be all right?"

"Sure, Doc." Denny Ray nodded cheerfully. "I bet I can beat you at checkers."

"I bet you can't. We'll see."

The procession filed out and as Ket left, she glanced at Denny Ray. He winked at her, and whispered, "Come and see me!"

Ket mouthed the words, "I will," and left.

Ketura was walking down the corridor, headed for the nurses' station when she heard Dr. Bjelland call out to her.

"Just a minute, Nurse Lindsey!"

She turned, took a steadying breath and waited for him to catch up. *What now?* she wondered with dread.

"I guess I was a bit hard on you back there in Denny Ray's room," he admitted gruffly.

"It's all right, Doctor. I was woolgathering. It won't happen again."

Bjelland stared at her. "You've always been my favorite new nurse. Maybe I haven't told you."

Ket's lips curled upward. "No, you haven't exactly overburdened me with compliments. That's not your way, though."

"No, it isn't." He hesitated then ran both hands through his shock of gray hair. "I'm worried about that boy Denny Ray."

"What's your real opinion?"

After listening carefully to a rather pessimistic report from Bjelland, Ket's heart sank. "You think it's that serious, then? He doesn't have any chance at all?"

"Of course he's got a chance. You believe in miracles, don't you?"

"Yes, I do."

Dr. Bjelland was himself an outspoken Christian, one of the few on the staff. "I do, too," he said. "We're going to do all we can. You, and I, and everybody else, but in the end I'm trusting God to do a work in this boy. We'll pray about that, won't we?"

"Yes, sir."

"All right, on your way."

When she reached the nursing station, Ket found Maggie and Debbie waiting. "Did he take your head off, honey?" Debbie grinned.

"No, not at all."

Maggie was staring at Ket. "What's wrong with you? You're supposed to be the most dedicated brain around here, and you're walking around like you're in a dense fog."

"I don't know," Ket said defensively. "Just thinking."

"You can't kid us." Debbie grinned impishly. "You've been in a daze all morning. I believe you've met somebody and won't tell. Come on now. Who is it?"

"I had the same feeling. Come on now, Ket. Tell," Maggie said.

The young women stared at her and Ket didn't know what to say. They were a close-knit group and two of the best friends Ket had in the world. Did she dare admit the thoughts that had been distracting her today?

Maggie suddenly lifted her head and narrowed her eyes. "Well, there he goes. Look at him. Is he a cutie or what?"

Ket lifted her glance and the other two followed suit. They watched as Jared Pierce walked by dressed in hospital greens.

"What was he like when you were in school with him, Ket?" Debbie asked.

"Well, he used to play baseball. I used to watch him play when we were in high school. He was an all-American at the University of Texas. I saw him play once on that team, too. When Texas won the national championship. He was a wonderful athlete."

The young women watched as the tall intern moved

on down the hall. "He's been dating Miss Texas," Ket remarked.

"You mean Lisa Glenn!" Debbie exclaimed. "She's beautiful!"

"Yes, everybody says she'll be Miss America this year," Maggie replied. She grinned suddenly and her eyes crinkled with amusement. "I think I'll take him away from her."

"You won't do that," Debbie replied. "He'd be crazy to turn her down." She snapped her fingers as if thinking of something new. "Did you know she's coming to the hospital this afternoon?" She tucked her hair under her snow-white cap, adding, "It's part of her duties as Miss Texas, I think. They do charitable things like that."

There was no time for more talk, for their duties called. Ket worked hard until two o'clock that afternoon when she took a break by visiting Denny Ray. He brightened up immediately when she entered the room, and said, "Have you got time to play a game of checkers?"

"Sure, but you better watch out. I feel mean this afternoon. Not giving anything away!"

However, Ket did give something away, for she managed to lose four games in a row and took great pleasure in watching Denny Ray's delight as he won.

"I guess I'm losing my touch," she said. "I'll have to figure out some better strategy."

Denny Ray grinned, his freckles standing out against his pale face. He looked thin and at times there was pain in his eyes as well as fear. "That's all right, Ket," he said. "I don't mind winning." He put the checkers carefully on the board for another game, then asked, "Where did you get a name like Ketura?"

"It comes from the Bible. Ketura was the second wife of Abraham."

"I bet the kids made fun of you when you were little."

"They still do." Ketura smiled. "However, there's one advantage. When somebody says, 'Hey, Ketura!' there's no question which Ketura they mean. Why, I think—"

She broke off abruptly for the doors had swung open. She rose quickly from the bed and moved over against the wall, for it seemed the room had suddenly become very crowded.

"Well, what is your name, little fellow?" a sugary voice inquired.

Ket had seen the Miss Texas contest on television and had been shocked at how Lisa had changed. She had been pretty enough in high school, but now she was fully mature—blond with green eyes and shaped as a Miss Texas ought to be, tall but with a curvy figure. She walked over to the bed and spoke in a honeyed voice, "My, aren't you a *nice* young man! I hope you're getting well from whatever's wrong with you."

Ket's eyes shot to Denny Ray's face. The young boy showed very little, but there was a flash of disdain in his eyes that Ket did not miss. "I'm fine," he said. "How are you?"

"Why, I'm just fine. Aren't you a perfect, little gentleman?"

Ket looked over to see a photographer, a short, round man with bushy black hair who at once began taking shots from every angle. The room seemed to explode with the flashes of light and Ket noticed that Lisa Glenn managed to turn her best side and a brilliant smile at the camera for every shot. Ket saw Jared Pierce standing in the doorway. He had not noticed her, she realized. Then the beauty queen began talking in a loud, rather artificially high voice—the type that some used with sick people when they know nothing else to do.

Suddenly Ket's eyes met his and he nodded briefly. She returned the nod and then she heard Lisa say, "Is there anything at all I can do for you, sweetie?"

Suddenly Denny Ray flashed a glimpse at Ket. A peculiar expression crossed his face and she knew he was up to something. "Sure," he said quickly. "Sit down and play a game of checkers with me."

Dismay swept across Lisa's flawless features. "Why, I'd—I'd love to, honey, but I have to go see some other patients. You know how it is?"

"Yeah, I know how it is," Denny Ray said evenly.

Ket turned her glance away from Lisa's bright smile to see a frown on the face of Dr. Jared Pierce. *He must know how phony she is,* Ket thought. But she had no time to think more, for the party prepared to head out for the next photographic appointment.

"Hello, Lisa," Ket said quietly.

"Why—Ket, it's *you!*" Lisa at once came over and hugged Ket, keeping her best side to the photographer. "Why, you haven't changed a bit! But what in the world are you doing here?"

"I'm on the nursing staff."

"Isn't that wonderful!" Lisa turned to wag a finger at Jared. "You didn't tell me Ket was working here."

"Guess I forgot."

"Well, shame on you for that, Jared Pierce! Why Ketura and I were pals in school, weren't we, Ket?" Ket was glad that Lisa did not wait for an answer from her, for the two of them had never been friends in any sense of the word. "Well, now, we'll have to get together, won't we? I'll call you."

"That would be nice," Ket said quietly, noting that Lisa didn't ask for her phone number. She watched as the small group was led out of the room by Lisa, then moved back over to stand beside Denny Ray. Ket smiled. "Well, you met a beauty queen. What did you think?"

"Boy, I feel sorry for the guy who gets stuck with her!"

Surprise swept across Ket's face. "Why do you say that?"

"Because she's a phony, that's why! She smiles with her teeth but not her eyes, and she talks too loud. And she called me *honey* and *sweetie* when she doesn't even know me."

"I think she meant well, Denny Ray."

"Sure, I guess so—but she's a phony for all of that."

Ket was amazed at the insight of the young man. She knew that his sickness had made him study people more carefully than most boys his age. "Well, I've got to go to work. Tell you what. Why don't I bring you a video tomorrow, and you and I will watch it."

"Good, I'm tired of these dumb cartoon shows. See if you can find an adventure story or something exciting."

Ket laughed. "I think I can handle that. I like a story with plenty of action, too."

She left the room then, and as she passed down the hall she heard the rather metallic laughter of Miss Texas drifting from an open doorway. She glanced in the room and saw the scene was being repeated. Only this time the patient was an elderly woman who was staring with shock at the beautiful, young girl who was telling her she was going to be fine.

"She's not going to be fine," Ket muttered between gritted teeth, "and it's not going to do any good for you to sweep in here telling people things like that." She was surprised at the strength of her emotion but then put it out of her mind as much as possible and went about her duties.

For the next four days Ket continued to feel an inner assurance that she was going to be married. She could not get the words or feelings out of her head. She dreamed about it, but still she found it almost impossible to believe.

"I'm becoming a basket case!" she muttered one

morning when she had lain awake for hours thinking about the Scripture and how ridiculous it might be for her God to be taking time to speak to her. "I just can't believe it's happening."

Still it went on, and more and more she began to be open to the concept that perhaps God was telling her something. "I've got to be very careful though. It would be so easy to make a big mistake," she cautioned herself. And she prayed for guidance and discernment. Prayer would keep her on the right path.

Chapter Four

The June sky was without a cloud, and the sun was hot as Ket cast her bait into the midst of a thick growth of water lilies. She let it lie there for ten seconds, counting slowly, then lifted her rod abruptly giving the plug a twitch. Instantly there was a thrashing in the lily pads and the line tightened, bringing the casting rod down level. Ket jerked the tip of the rod upward, sinking the hook and yelling at the top of her lungs, "I've got him, Dad! I've got him!"

"Hey, watch out! You're going to turn the boat over!" Roger Lindsey sat in the front of the bass boat and laughed aloud as he watched Ket fight to pull the fish out of the lily pads.

"You'll never get him in. He's going to get hung up," he said. He watched as she skillfully worked the fish, and thought, *She's a better fisherman than I am. Better than most men.* Aloud, he said, "I never saw anybody get so excited over a little thing like a fish. One of these days you're going to jump right out of the boat and haul yourself over to a bass, hand over hand."

Ket did not answer for, as always, she had a mild form of insanity when she got a fish hooked, especially a large fellow like this one. It seemed the whole world disappeared, and all she knew was the tug of the fish on her line, the splashing of the water and the fish's mad attempt to escape.

"He's a whale, Dad!" Ket yelled. "Maybe a record!"

Roger watched with amusement and pride as Ket worked the fish close to the boat, then reached out quickly, grabbed the landing net and slipped it under the fish. When she lifted it out of the water, he whistled, "Say, that is a big fish! He might go eight or nine pounds!"

Ket looked down to see that her hands were trembling. "Look at that! I'm not going to make much of a nurse if I get all shaky over a little thing like a fish." She reached in and got the fish by the underjaw and lifted him out. Her father came quickly with the scales and hooked it into the fish's jaw, then waited until he stopped thrashing. "Eight and three quarter pounds! That's a fine bass! Be good for supper tonight."

"No, I'm going to have him mounted. We can get some fish at the supermarket."

"He *would* make a nice trophy. Look at those colors!" Roger said admiringly. The two carefully put the fish into a wire basket and lowered him so that he would live as long as possible.

"Let's go home," Ket said. "Anything after this would be an anticlimax."

"Suits me. Time we get by Ed's house and let him start on your fish. It'll be getting late anyhow."

The two got their gear stowed and Ket moved to the driver's seat. She started the powerful engine and soon the boat was skimming across Runaway Bay.

"I love to come out here," she shouted with the roar of the engine.

"You ought to come more. Both of us should."

"All right, it's a date."

Ket and her father parked the boat in their marina and soon were on their way home. They stopped off to give the fish to the taxidermist, Ed Jennings, and he promised to have it mounted in a few days.

Roger pulled onto the main road and headed home. He glanced across the seat at his daughter, who looked tired but content. Her hair was blowing in the wind from the open windows and he thought again how much she looked like him. *I should wish she were small, petite and beautiful like her sisters and Lucille— but this one is mine.* After a moment, he said, "How's it going at the hospital?"

"Oh, fine." She hesitated and then said, "I'm worried about one of our patients, a ten-year-old boy. He has a bad heart problem."

"He's not doing well?"

"No—not at all."

"What chance does he have?"

"I don't know, Dad. I talked to Dr. Bjelland, but he

won't come right out and say. I don't think he's very hopeful though, and he's such a sweet boy."

"That's tough. It's hard to hear about anybody that sick, but when it's a ten-year-old, that really gets to your heart, doesn't it?"

Suddenly Ket remembered the visit by Lisa Glenn, and she gave her father a summary. Indignantly, she said, "She didn't care about Denny Ray. She was too busy posing for the camera."

"That's pretty harsh coming from you, Ket."

Ket flushed and ran her hand through her hair. "I know, but it was so obvious. Denny Ray knew what she was doing right away. He said so as soon as she left."

"Well, at least he's got you on his side." He changed the subject, saying, "Did you know that she's going to be in church tomorrow?"

"Who's going to be in church tomorrow?" Ket asked, turning her gaze on him.

"Why, Miss Texas. Guess you didn't read the bulletin last week."

"Lisa's going to be there?"

"Yes, going to talk about her charity work."

Sighing deeply, Ket sank down in her seat. "I guess I'll go, but I don't like it."

The next morning Ketura found the large sanctuary at her church packed, for as Ket discovered everyone knew that Miss Texas would be here. She had threatened again not to go, but her father had been firm about that, and knowing he was right, she came reluctantly.

And now as the song service went on, she examined Miss Texas very carefully.

Lisa Glenn sat in the front pew, right in front of the minister's pulpit. She was wearing a beautifully tailored cream-colored jacket with long sleeves and gold-tone buttons. The matching straight skirt came to just below her knees and she had on a pair of shoes with high heels of the same color.

She does look beautiful, Ket thought reluctantly. *It's almost unfair that a woman could be that much better looking than other women.*

Her gaze shifted to Jared Pierce who sat beside Lisa. He was wearing a tan sports coat, a white shirt and a maroon tie. His auburn hair seemed to catch the light, and Ket thought, *He's almost as attractive as she is. They certainly make a nice-looking couple.*

Finally the song service ended and the senior pastor, William Arlen, came to the front. Ketura always enjoyed Pastor Arlen's sermons but noticed that he was not going to speak today. It seemed that a minister who was on the faculty of a local seminary had been invited to address the congregation. "It's an honor for me to introduce our next guest," Pastor Arlen said. "She is Miss Texas as you know, and we are convinced that she will be Miss America."

Ket was rather disgusted to hear the congregation applaud. *Who cares if she's going to be Miss America?* Ket was, however, accustomed to athletes and beauty queens being honored. It always gave her a stab of dismay, for she knew that God did not look on the outside of people. She was well aware that some of the best servants and the most devoted Christians in the church were not the stars on the football team or those elected beauty queen, but people who never received much recognition.

"And now I want you to give a good welcome to Lisa Glenn, Miss Texas."

Again there was applause, but Ket did not join in. She exchanged glances with her father, her lips tight, and shrugged as if to say, "Well, that's the way it is. No sense fighting it."

"I am so happy to be here, for it is always a joy to visit with my friends in the church. It's highly important that we give a day to God, for He deserves it...." Lisa was bubbly, and her smile flashed constantly. She spoke of using her celebrity to help various charities and bring attention to those in need, but it all sounded so rehearsed and shallow to Ketura. Ket had already seen Lisa in action at the hospital and knew that her efforts were insincere, an endless photo shoot.

"Thank you so much, Miss Glenn," the pastor said. "And now we have another honored guest, Mr. Jared Pierce." Ketura felt surprised. She had no idea Jared was going to speak. "As some of you who are baseball fans may know, Mr. Pierce was all-American shortstop at the University of Texas. An injury, unfortunately, caught up with him, but there are those who say he would have been one of the best players in the major league right now if he had been able. He is an intern at

Mercy Hospital. Jared, come and tell people what God's done in your life."

There was only a splattering of applause this time. As Jared came to stand behind the pulpit, he looked somehow awkward and ill at ease. Ket heard a young girl behind her, whispering, "Isn't he the handsomest thing you ever saw?" She resisted the impulse to turn around and shush her. Instead, she sat quietly in her pew and waited for the testimony.

Jared had a pleasant baritone voice and despite his initial awkwardness, he quickly took command of himself. "I appreciate the opportunity to share with you what Jesus Christ has done in my life. I appreciate what the pastor said about my baseball-playing days. I think it was the darkest day in my life, when a doctor looked at me, and said, 'Your days of playing ball are over.'" He looked down for a moment and seemed lost in thought. There was something sad about him, Ket realized, and she thought, *That must have been horrible for him! He was so good and to lose it all...*

Jared looked up again and smiled. "I couldn't play ball so I decided to become a doctor, and I must tell you it is a wonderful thing to be given a second chance at another career." He went on to speak to them earnestly about the lesson he learned—if you could not achieve your life dream, then take what God puts in your way. He referred to the story of Joseph more than once, saying, "Joseph was a man who had everything going, but it was all taken away from him. But he never gave up. Even in prison he kept his faith in his God.

So I would encourage you this morning to keep your faith in Jesus Christ always before you. Even when things have gone wrong when you don't understand what God is saying, keep on believing in our Savior. Allow Him to show you the way. Thank you very much."

Ket felt strangely warm as she whispered to her father, "That was a fine testimony."

"Yes, it was. Not flashy, but honest and down-to-earth. He seems a strange match for Lisa Glenn. She's rather superficial, and I think that young man's got something in him."

The sermon that morning was by Dr. Albert Jones, a professor of Old Testament at a seminary. He was an excellent scholar, and as an experienced preacher he had an impressive delivery. When he announced his subject, Ket immediately sat straighter. The subject was "How To Know the Will of God."

Ket sat there expectantly, almost leaning forward. *That's what I need to find out—how to know the will of God, and especially if you can know it directly.*

But Ket was doomed to disappointment. After exploring many ways of knowing God's will, such as through the Scripture, and through the counsel of friends, and through the teachers that God sent your way, finally Dr. Jones said almost sadly, "Unfortunately God does not speak directly in our days. He did, of course, in the old days, before we had the Bible, but now we must depend on the means at hand. I know many who ruin their lives by seeking to hear directly from God, and I would caution you not to fall into this trap."

As Ket left the church, she was deeply depressed. The sermon was not what she wanted to hear, and she asked herself, *Can this be right? If Dr. Jones is right, then I'm wrong, and all of this turmoil I'm going through is just a psychological phenomenon.*

"Are you all right, Ket?" her mother asked.

"Yes, Mom."

"You look a little disappointed. Didn't you like the preacher?"

"Oh, he was fine," Ket replied quickly, but inside there was an echo that saddened her. Her faith had been shaken.

Kirk Delgado was one of the second-year interns. He almost shocked Ket to her shoe tops when he stopped by her nursing station on Thursday and said casually, "How about you and I go out to dinner?"

"What did you say, Kirk?"

"I'm asking you for a date." Kirk was a handsome, young man of twenty-six, with dark hair and eyes. Everyone knew he got by on charm more than on his intellect. He was determined to be a dermatologist, because, as he often said, "Patients never call after hours, they never get well, and they never die. What more can you ask?"

Most of the young women that Ket knew in the hospital had gone out with him at one time or another, but he had never asked her. She said quickly, "I don't think so, Kirk."

"Oh, come on! There's a revival of *The Music Man* on. You like musicals, don't you?"

As a matter of fact, Ket was very fond of old musicals, such as *Singing in the Rain, The Music Man* and *My Fair Lady.* She had been intending to go to see the revival of *The Music Man* for it starred one of her favorite actors. Still, she said wearily, "Oh, I don't know…."

"Hey, come on, it'll do you good!" His smile was warm and coaxing. "We'll go to a nice steak house and then see *The Music Man.* Be a good break for you."

Ket thought briefly about her resolve to have no more dates, but finally decided Kirk was harmless. "Well, all right. What time?"

"I'll pick you up at six. The show doesn't start until eight."

All afternoon Ket worried about what she had done. She had nothing against Kirk except he was a rather frivolous young man, but somehow it seemed wrong. When she mentioned the date to Maggie Stone, her friend's eyes suddenly glittered. "So, Kissing Kirk has finally gotten around to you. Watch yourself with that one."

Instantly Ket looked up. "What do you mean?"

"You know what I mean. He's too fresh, and he thinks he's the greatest thing that ever happened to womankind. I'm surprised you'd even think of dating him. But that's a good show. Just take a blackjack along—or a cattle prod!"

Maggie's words disturbed Ket, and she regretted

having agreed to go out with Kirk. However, what was done was done, and as she left work that afternoon, she shrugged to herself, saying, "Well, it's just one evening."

She had time to get her hair fixed, and then went home and dressed for the date. Her mother smiled as she came down the stairs. "My, don't you look nice! I've always liked that dress," Lucille said.

Ketura smiled. The dress was one of her favorites, too. It was simple and elegantly shaped, slightly fitted and very feminine. It had a round neck, was sleeveless, and came to touch just above her knees. The deep coral color complemented her blond hair and fair skin.

"Who is this fellow?" Roger asked. "Do I know him?"

"Oh, he's one of the second-year interns. I've known him for about a year," Ket replied.

Promptly at six the doorbell rang and Roger answered it. He introduced himself and shook hands with Kirk. Kirk was wearing a pair of charcoal slacks and a tan sports coat. He charmed Ket's mother, then said quickly, "I guess we'd better get started. We've got a busy night. We might be a little late, I'm afraid, but don't worry, I'll take care of her."

Ket was not surprised that Kirk drove a fancy sports car. It was flashy, fire-engine red and she had to hear all about it as they drove to the restaurant. He was surprised that she knew as much about engines or more than he did and laughed, saying, "Not only a nurse, but a connoisseur of sports cars. That's unusual."

Their dinner at the restaurant Kirk had chosen was

good and Ket ate her meal heartily. She did a lot of listening, and soon she heard Kirk saying, "You know, Ket, I've fallen a little bit behind with my studies. I was wondering if you would help me catch up."

Ket answered quickly, "Why sure. Anything I can do." She listened and quickly discovered the reason why Kirk had asked her out. He was due for his exams, and what he really wanted was for someone to tutor him so that he could pass.

"It'd be fun. We could spend a lot of time together. You're the smartest nurse in the whole hospital, so the rumor goes." He grinned and looked very handsome as he leaned across the table. He stopped and took her hand, and said, "You tutor me and I'll take you to musicals and feed you steaks."

Ket felt used, but did not make a scene. "I'll be glad to help some, but my time's a little bit limited, Kirk."

A petulant, disappointed look crossed his face and Ket could see he was not used to being turned away by women. But he soon grinned, saying, "I'll talk you into it. You just wait."

The Music Man was a delight, and Ket enjoyed the production thoroughly. They left the theater a little after eleven and Ket talked freely about the performance all the way home.

When they pulled up in front of the driveway Ketura thanked him for the evening and started to get out of the car. Kirk quickly reached over and pulled her close to him. Before she could protest, he kissed her so hard she couldn't breath. Finally she pulled away.

"Stop that, Kirk!"

"Aw, come on, what's a little kiss?"

"I'm sorry, but I've got to go in."

"Wait a minute!" Kirk protested, but Ket got out of his car and slammed the door. She was nearly to the house when he reached her and turned her around. "What's the matter with you, Ket?"

"Nothing's the matter with me! Let me go, Kirk!"

"Aw, you don't mean that." He tried to pull her closer, but she pushed him in the chest and ran to the front door.

Kirk stared up at her as she unlocked the door. He was angry clear through. "You're just an iceberg! That's what they say about you. Nothing but a chunk of ice!"

Ket stepped inside and wanted to slam the door. She was breathing hard and anger rushed through her. Not wanting to awaken her parents, she tiptoed down the hall, went into her room and then discovered she was trembling. With unsteady hands she removed her earrings and then undressed. She didn't bother taking a shower but slipped into her pajamas and got into bed. Her mind was crowded with thoughts. *I never should have gone with him—I knew what he was like and I went anyway. What's wrong with me?*

Finally she remembered that she had not read the Scripture as she had promised herself to do every night. Turning on the light, she fluffed up a pillow, sat up and pulled the Bible from the night table. She read one of the Psalms but could not make herself be still. Finally she shut the Bible and slammed it down, and then turned the light out. Almost violently she put her head down, punched the pillow and said, "All right, I'll just be a spinster! I'll never get married."

She lay awake for a long time in confusion and she had a few tears, then finally drifted off to sleep.

She did not know what time it was, but it was very dark. It must have been three o'clock, at least. She did not even open her eyes fully to look at the luminous glow of the clock at her bedside, for she knew that somehow God had wakened her. As she lay there, at last calm but still disturbed over the date, she said aloud, "God, I'm sorry I wasted this night."

For a long time she lay there praying and thanking God for her blessings, and finally she said, "I must have missed You, God. I surely couldn't have heard you right."

She lay there waiting on the Lord for some sort of message, and finally it came. It came very oddly.

Have you forgotten My promise? You will have a husband—if you will believe me.

Ketura lay absolutely still. She let the impression sink into her spirit, and finally she murmured, "All right. I don't want to limit You, Lord. I'll believe You no matter how foolish the thing You want me to do sounds." And then she prayed what she knew for most people is the hardest prayer of all—"Thy will be done!"

Chapter Five

Jared saw Nurse Helen Gantry, the dark-haired supervisor, moving around the floor in her familiar, efficient manner. He was surprised, however, to see Ketura Lindsey following close behind. As far as he knew, she'd never been scheduled in the E.R., and he'd never worked with her before. He'd heard that she was a good nurse—calm, caring and knowledgeable. That didn't surprise him. He remembered Ket being very bright in school. Her intelligence had been a bit intimidating in fact, along with her height and a certain aloof manner, telling the world she was her own person and didn't care what anyone thought of her. The combination had put boys off, he recalled. Though now he questioned if she was really so haughty, or simply shy. He wondered if they'd be teamed up to work on any patients tonight and soon got his answer when two paramedics wheeled in a man who had been hurt in a car accident.

"Dr. Pierce, room three," Helen Gantry directed him.

Jared entered the exam room and washed his hands at the sink as the paramedics transferred the patient to a table. Nurse Gantry soon returned to the room followed by Ket. She glanced over at him, looking surprised to see him there, Jared thought. "Hello, Ket. Looks like we drew the same shift," he greeted her.

"Looks like it. They were shorthanded here tonight so I was told to come down."

Jared dried his hands and smiled at her. She looked a little nervous, he thought, but he didn't have a chance to say more. Ket quickly turned away and focused on the patient, doing her part to stabilize him and read his vital signs. Helen stood at the other side of the bed, taking a history while Ket checked his pulse and blood pressure.

Jared stepped over and stared down at the middle-aged man. Conscious, no visible bleeding, though there could be some internally. Obviously in pain, Jared noted.

"George Reynolds, age forty-six," Helen said. "Car accident. Says he has no preexisting conditions, but he's complaining of pain in his head and stomach."

"Have you sent to X-ray for a portable?"

"It's on the way," Ket reported.

"What's the blood pressure?"

"Ninety over eighty-two," Ket replied. "The guys in the ambulance said it was even lower before the Plasmanate kicked in. Pulse is a hundred and forty-two."

Jared met the patient's gaze and managed a tired smile. "I'm Dr. Pierce, Mr. Reynolds. I'm going to take a look at you. See what's going on."

The man looked terrified but submitted to Jared's examination. Jared then quickly and methodically examined the patient's head, eyes, ears, nose, mouth and moved the jaws. He asked the patient questions, then examined his ribs and stomach.

"He needs a Lebvine," Jared said turning to Ket. She nodded and disappeared.

George Reynolds looked alarmed and tried to sit up, but his stomach pain was too intense. "What are you doing to me? I want my own doctor...."

Jared rested a steadying hand on the patient's shoulder and eased him back down again. "We'll get your doctor, Mr. Reynolds, as soon as we can. You can go to any hospital you please. But right now you're here with me, and I've got to do what I can to help you."

At that moment, Ket reappeared with the apparatus he'd asked for. "Will a number eighteen be okay, Dr. Pierce? You didn't specify."

"That's perfect. Thanks." *I knew she'd be sharp,* Jared thought. As Ket began to lubricate the tip of the tube, he turned to the patient.

"Now, I'm going to have to put this tube into your stomach, Mr. Reynolds. We need to extract the fluid that's collecting there." Jared took the tube and held out the tip toward the patient. "It will feel uncomfortable at first, but this will be much easier if you relax."

The patient stared back at Jared with a puzzled expression for a moment, then jerked his head away. "Go away! You're not sticking that thing up my nose! What kind of place is this?"

Jared stared back at him. He'd worked with enough different patients by now to know when a firm hand was needed. With some you needed great gentleness and tact, but this man was obviously not that kind.

"Look, man, you don't get it. You're seriously injured. I'm trying to save your life. This is a stomach pump—it's a very simple procedure."

He tried again to insert the tip of the tube into the patient's nose, but the man knocked his hand away. He heard Ketura standing behind him. "Shall I call the orderlies to help you?"

Jared shook his head. Keeping his frustration under control, he tried again. "Mr. Reynolds, you need this tube. It'd be easier if you were unconscious or even sedated, but I'd rather not administer sedatives until we know the extent of your injuries. Now, this isn't fun. I agree. But if you don't let me carry on this procedure, you may die. Do you understand me?"

The man stared back at him, still belligerent. Finally, Jared saw him give in. This time, when Jared held out the tube, he didn't get pushed away and Jared proceeded, carefully sliding the tube through the nose, down the throat, into the man's stomach, then secured the other end of the tubing to the plastic suction canister that was attached to a wall.

Reynolds lay still as a mummy, apparently frightened into submission. A technician arrived with the portable X-ray machine and Ketura led him over to the patient's bed.

Jared leaned over the patient and touched his arm. "They're going to take pictures of your stomach and head, so we can tell what's really going on. I'll be back in a little while to see how you're doing."

He saw Reynolds swallow hard, and then he nodded.

The X-ray technician stepped in and started his work. Jared turned to go and met Ketura at the door. "He's a tough customer," she noted. "Looks like you got him under control, though."

Jared grinned at her. "I usually try a little more bedside manner before resorting to the scare tactics, but it's been a long day."

She cast him a weary smile and he knew she understood completely. "There's a lot of action down here tonight. It makes my floor look like a library."

Jared laughed. "I'm sure your watch up there isn't quite that easy, Ketura."

She shrugged, her blue-gray eyes sparkling. "I don't like it too quiet. I like to use what I've learned. I didn't spend all those years in school to sit filling out charts."

"No...I can see that's not your style." Jared wasn't surprised. Ketura Lindsey had enough vitality and spirit for three nurses, and he realized that he'd enjoyed working with her on their ornery patient. No, *enjoyed* wasn't quite the right word, Jared thought. It was more like feeling secure, knowing he had strong backup, a calm, intelligent right-hand person. That should have been the way with all nurses, but unfortunately it was not.

He smiled at her and noticed how she smiled back a moment, then seemed suddenly self-conscious and shyly looked away, a dash of color rising in her fair complexion.

He was about to say goodbye and head off, but sensed Ketura wanted to say something more. "Listen…I never got to thank you for the other day. With Dr. Bjelland," she said. "I really wasn't paying attention to him. I deserved to be blasted. You didn't have to make an excuse for me."

It took Jared a moment to recall the incident. Then all he could remember was the startled, embarrassed look on Ketura's face and the jeering of his fellow interns. He couldn't have stood by and not helped her. It just wasn't his nature.

"Bjelland's a fine doctor, but sometimes he's a rude idiot. He shouldn't have embarrassed you like that. You're not even under his supervision…. Besides, I definitely heard that cleaning cart," he added with a crooked grin. "I guess you missed it."

Ketura smiled back at him, glancing down shyly again in a way he found very charming.

"Yes…I must have."

Suddenly they both heard Jared's name summoned on the PA system. "Someone's looking for me. Catch you later," he added, heading down the hall.

"Sure. See you." Ketura nodded and turned back to her own duties.

Jared checked his watch as he headed toward his next case. Two hours to go. The tail end of the shift usually passed quickly, though by now he was very tired and had to be mindful of making mistakes. He worked hard and didn't stop to think about anything except patients.

Finally, he was relieved by Kirk Delgado, who came in breezily thirty minutes late and didn't even apologize. While scrubbing up Kirk glanced over at Jared. "Busy night?"

"Always busy down here."

Kirk scowled. "I don't see how the emergency room is going to help me. Dermatologists don't have to visit emergency rooms."

Jared didn't argue with him. Emergency or not, Jared pitied the poor patients who got stuck with Kirk. He knew his fellow intern was careless in his procedures and shaky in his knowledge of medicine. It was some consolation that Kirk had not chosen brain surgery as his specialty, Jared thought. Some…but not much.

"Hey, Jared, do you know that tall nurse with the funny name?"

Jared frowned. He didn't like the demeaning way Kirk described Ketura and answered in a brusque tone. "Ketura Lindsey. Is that who you mean?"

"Yeah, that's the one. I just saw her on the floor. She's not working down here tonight, is she?"

Kirk sounded nervous, Jared noticed, though being such a sloppy doctor, he'd be lucky to have Ketura watching over his shoulder.

"She just finished the shift.... What's the matter, Kirk? Did she turn you down?"

"Me? No way, man. The ladies never turn me down." Kirk laughed arrogantly, tugging a surgical green shirt over his head. "I took her out the other night. What a bore. I don't know why I even bothered."

Jared smiled to himself. He wasn't surprised that a woman with Ket's brains had baffled Kirk. But he was surprised to hear that she'd agreed to date their local Lothario. Kirk must have nagged her endlessly.

"I just don't understand women," Kirk complained. "They drive me crazy. But I guess dating a beauty queen, you don't need to keep looking around. It's hard work, man."

Jared shook his head and buttoned up his shirt. "Don't you think about anything but women, Kirk?"

Kirk stared at him, looking amazed at the question. "Oh, like my patients and being a doctor and all that?"

Jared nodded. "For example."

Kirk laughed and closed his locker. "Sure, sometimes. But I try not to let that heavy stuff distract me too much." He winked at Jared and jauntily left for the floor. "See you, Pierce."

"Yeah, see you." Relieved to be alone once more, he quickly finished dressing.

Jared left the hospital and stepped into the cool night air. He felt beat and wished he could just snap his fingers and find himself stretched out on his sofa in front of the TV. He knew if he closed his eyes for one second, he'd most likely fall asleep. But he'd planned to meet Lisa tonight and scanned the parking lot for her sleek new sports car, a gift from her doting father.

He didn't have to look for long. No sooner had he stepped off the curb than he heard the insistent beep of a car horn. He glanced around and found her parked in the Doctors Only zone. The convertible top on her car was down and she waved and beeped again, making sure he saw her.

"You said eight o'clock. I've been waiting for ages," Lisa greeted him. "I nearly gave up." Jared got inside, then briefly kissed her cheek before clipping his seat belt.

"I'm sorry. It was a long shift. Delgado came in late and I had to wait for him."

"Well, we can still get something to eat." Lisa glanced over at him, finally smiling.

"That sounds good. Anyplace you like." Jared was so hungry and tired, he really didn't care where they went.

"I'll think of someplace fun," she promised.

Weaving in and out of traffic, Lisa managed to break half the traffic laws in Texas as she made her way to her favorite steak house. They finally arrived and she pulled into a parking slot that said Manager. Jared glanced at her but she smiled and shrugged. "He's probably gone home by now. Come on. Let's just go in. I'm starved."

They went inside, and Lisa soon charmed the hostess into giving them the best table in the house. She ordered a T-bone steak and Jared selected barbecued chicken. As he sat listening to Lisa talk excitedly about her activities, he had to focus his attention to take it all in.

"You're not listening to me, Jared," she complained.

"Sure I am."

"No, you're not. I can tell." She had raised pouting to a fine art, Jared thought, and did so now, leaning back in her chair and giving him a look. The pouting act didn't have much effect on him lately though, not the way it used to, and she seemed to sense this. Changing her tact, she leaned forward and put her hand on his. "Why don't you take a few days off? You can travel with me. I'm scheduled to speak everywhere. It would be a nice break for you."

"I'd like to, Lisa," he began slowly. "But you know I can't get time off from the hospital."

"Oh…! The hospital," she echoed with exasperation.

"Where are you going?" he asked, hoping to distract her.

"Tomorrow I'm going to Houston. To talk to a political group. Doesn't that sound like fun?"

"You don't even like politics," Jared said with a laugh. "What will you talk about?" He hadn't meant to laugh, but the idea was amusing. Lisa made no secret of the fact that she was bored silly by anything even remotely resembling the news or current events.

"They want me to talk about becoming Miss America, of course."

"Yes, of course." Jared's tone was kinder, but he could see she felt slighted. "You're working awfully hard for this contest, Lisa. I hope you win it."

Anger touched her eyes, and a sullen expression came to her lips. "Of course I'll win it. You're always so negative lately, Jared. Why don't you have more faith in me? Why, it's the most important thing that's ever happened in my life. I wish you could be more supportive. I can do so much good if I become Miss America, you know."

He was only trying to be objective about it. Realistic, actually. He hadn't meant to hurt her feelings. But they just didn't think the same way, Jared reminded himself.

"Of course I want you to win," he assured her. "Don't mind me. I'm really tired."

She pouted again for a moment, but soon launched off into more talk about her publicity appearances. Jared listened, tried to follow, but his thoughts drifted.

Could she do a lot of good if she became Miss America? Jared wanted to give her the benefit of the doubt, but he really couldn't say for sure. The last year or so, Lisa had really changed. Or maybe *he* had changed? He couldn't say for sure about that, either. But something definitely felt different lately, out of sync from the way it used to be.

When he'd first started dating Lisa, she was the prettiest girl he'd ever seen, and every guy he knew wanted to go out with her. For some reason, she'd chosen him. Maybe because he didn't chase her. He'd felt like a grand-prize winner and couldn't believe his good luck. Sure, she'd been a cheerleader and prom queen, but back then, she'd had some goals and interests beyond posing for cameras or seeing herself on TV and in the movies. She'd studied education in college and had wanted to be a teacher. She'd even completed her course work, but had never followed through on other requirements like student teaching. Lisa claimed she just didn't have the time since the extra work cut into her run for the Miss Texas t...e. Now he never heard a word about a career as a teacher, he realized, and he wondered if he ever would again.

Lisa had once had other interests that he hadn't heard anything about recently, either. Unless she was being interviewed, of course. Volunteer work, like visiting seniors and tutoring kids who didn't have enough support with school work at home. Those pursuits had gone by the wayside, too. She hardly even went to church anymore as far as he knew, unless she was asked to be a speaker.

Lisa had always been a bit vain, but what young woman with her looks wouldn't be? Jared accepted that about her and knew it came with the package. But now it seemed to him there was nothing *but* a package. A beautifully wrapped gift, with nothing inside. How had that happened? He had to say that, years ago, she'd just been a nicer person, with more meaningful goals... more meaningful values. She'd been easier to please and sweeter somehow. Now she seemed so demanding and calculating. He sometimes found it a shock and knew he'd been hiding his head in the sand, preferring to ignore these changes in her personality rather than face the truth.

He realized that, for so long, he'd been waiting. Hoping it was all just a phase, because of these beauty pageants and all the attention. But now it seemed clear to him. Lisa would never be the girl he once knew. Not after the pageant, not after she got a role in a movie or on TV. Not ever. Either this was her real self, coming into full bloom, or the pursuit of these goals—which in all honesty seemed so shallow and meaningless to him—had changed her in some fundamental way.

I'm not happy in this relationship anymore, Jared thought, *and neither is she. Not really.* He stared at her and sighed, then realized that Lisa had asked him a question and was waiting for an answer.

"Excuse me? I didn't hear you," he apologized.

She shook her head with frustration and sighed. "I asked if you wanted to check out that new club, Sparks. It's just down the road from here. Some of my friends are going. There might be a line outside, but I'm sure someone will recognize me and give us priority."

Jared stared at her blankly. A noisy, crowded club was the last place he wanted to be right now. Didn't she understand how tired he felt? How his day had been long and stressful and how he faced another one, just like it, tomorrow?

"I don't think I'm up for that tonight, Lisa. Too beat. Sorry," he said with a small smile.

Lisa's green eyes narrowed and she frowned at him.

"I knew you'd say that. You never feel like doing anything fun anymore. I hardly even get to see you, and when we do get together…well, you just sit there, looking practically catatonic."

Bored into a coma by all the pageant talk, Jared wanted to reply. But he gallantly held his tongue and tried to make light of her criticism. "I'm an intern. I'm supposed to be catatonic. That's part of the training."

"Don't make a joke out of this, Jared. It's serious." Lisa's tone rose on a shrill note. A couple sitting nearby turned and gave them a look. Jared felt embarrassed.

If she doesn't understand the demands of my profession now, what will happen if we ever get married? he thought. Maybe this was the right moment to bring up his doubts about their future. She seemed to have plenty of her own, too, he realized.

He nodded. "Yes, it is serious…. You're right."

He stared at her, about to speak, but the waiter arrived to deliver the bill, interrupting the moment. Jared glanced at the paper quickly and pulled out some cash from his wallet. When he looked back at Lisa, she'd already collected her purse and taken out her car keys, prepared to go. He pulled out her chair and walked behind her as she stalked angrily to her car. They drove in silence to his apartment house, where she parked by the curb, the motor running.

"Well, good night." He leaned over and kissed her, but she stared straight ahead, as responsive as a block of stone. He got out of the car and shut the door. "Drive home safely."

She glanced at him with a mischievous smile and flipped her long hair back with her hand. "I'm not going home yet. It's still early. I think I'll go meet my friends at that club…. You don't mind, do you?"

Was she trying to make him jealous? He would have been at one time. Oddly, he didn't feel that way now. He didn't feel much of anything. Not a good sign, either, he realized.

Jared stepped back from the car and shrugged. "You don't need my permission. Sure…go ahead. See your friends. Have fun."

His agreeable response displeased her. Her pretty face set in a scowl, she turned to the road and gunned the engine.

"Don't worry. *I will.*"

Before he could respond, the sports car peeled away from the curb and sped down the street. Jared stood on the sidewalk and watched until she disappeared. He and Lisa had argued before. That was nothing new. But this time it felt like a turning point.

He had started to face his real feelings tonight, bringing him relief in some way and in another, deep sadness.

As Ket neared Denny Ray's room, she realized she had been on automatic all day, carrying out her duties but on automatic. She had thought all day about the message she'd heard inside and how she had promised God to believe Him no matter how foolish it seemed.

Now, as Ket entered the room, she forced all

thoughts of the "voice" out of her mind and moved over to greet Denny Ray. "How are you doing today, champ?"

"Not so good." Denny Ray's voice was weak and he was, indeed, pale and lacking his usual smile.

Moving over to stand beside him, Ket reached out and smoothed his blond hair back from his forehead. "Not too good, eh?"

"Not very."

For a small boy who was so sick and frightened, she knew being alone so much must be awful. "Are your mom and dad coming in today?"

"Mom is. Dad's still up in Canada. I wish he was here."

"I wish he were, too." Ket thought of Bill Kelland and his wife, Ellen, Denny Ray's parents. They had been older than most when Denny Ray had been born and they were very protective. Ellen Kelland was very dependent upon her husband, but his work in construction often kept him away. He flew in from Canada every weekend, but now Ket wished both parents were here.

"Do you want to play checkers?"

"Don't feel good enough."

Ket stood beside the boy's bed praying desperately for something to say, but what do you say to a young boy who lives in the shadow of death and who knows it? She saw the raw fear now in his eyes, and she leaned forward and took his hand. He grabbed at her with both of his and held on tightly.

"Are you afraid, Denny Ray?" she whispered.

His lower lip trembled and he bit it for a moment. "Yeah...sometimes," he admitted.

Ket leaned closer and put her arm around his thin shoulders. "We all feel afraid sometimes. We all feel like giving up. Even grown-ups, who seem like they have it all figured out and know everything, feel that way sometimes."

Denny Ray met her glance for a moment. "Even Dr. Bjelland?"

Ket gently smiled. "Yes...even big, scary Dr. Bjelland, but don't tell him I told you, okay? I have a feeling he wouldn't want that getting around. It might ruin his image."

"Yeah, I know what you mean." Denny Ray smiled for a moment. Then she saw his expression darken again. She heard him sigh and she sighed, too, praying for the right words to soothe his fears, to give him comfort and hope.

"Do you know what I do when I feel afraid? What Dr. Bjelland does, too," she added.

"Think of something happy or something like that?" Denny Ray's tone was almost cynical, and Ketura sensed he'd had this conversation before.

"Not exactly. Sometimes I like to read my Bible. To read stories about other people who've faced a hard time and gotten through it. With God's help."

"I guess I've read the Bible a few times. In Sunday school, mostly. It seemed sort of boring," he said honestly. "I don't see how that would help me much. Besides, I don't even have one around."

Ketura had noticed that. "Well, besides reading the Bible, there's another thing I do when I feel scared. I talk to God. I tell Him about my problems, whatever's troubling me. I ask for His help."

Denny Ray glanced at her curiously. "Does He answer you?"

She nodded. "Yes. He does. Sometimes it's just a feeling I get. Sometimes, it's stronger, as if I hear Him talking back, in my head. But He does answer, and He always helps. And talking to Him always makes me feel better. Not afraid anymore." Ketura reached up and touched Denny Ray's soft blond hair. "God really loves you, Denny Ray. He loves you very much."

Denny Ray sat looking straight ahead, but he seemed to be considering her words very seriously, she thought. Finally he glanced over at her again. "I don't go to church much. Only sometimes with my Mom. I know a few prayers, though."

"Would you like to say a prayer together?" Ketura asked gently.

Denny Ray nodded. "How about The Lord's Prayer? I know that one."

"Yes, of course. Why don't you start it." Ketura clasped her hands and bowed her head, and Denny Ray did the same. He started the prayer, and Ketura recited along with him, listening as Denny Ray stumbled only once over the words.

When they were done, he looked up at her, his expression somewhat calmer. "I guess I'd like to talk to God a little now. You know, like you said, in my own way."

Ketura sat back. "Would you like me to go so you can talk privately?"

Denny Ray considered her offer for a second, then shook his head. "That's okay. You can stay. It won't take long."

Ketura was touched by the boy's trust. It was such a sweet compliment to hear that he didn't mind her listening in. She only hoped that his private words to God didn't set off her tears.

Denny Ray bowed his head and clasped his hands again. "Dear God. It's me, Denny Ray Kelland. I guess You know I'm pretty sick. I'd sure like to get better. I'd do just about anything to be out playing baseball again with the other kids. Or riding my bike. Sometimes I'm afraid I'll never do that kind of stuff anymore…. Sometimes I'm scared I might really die. And I don't want to. I know that You can do anything. So would You please help me get better really soon? Ket says You love me…. I love You, too."

He remained with his head bowed a moment longer. Ketura watched, swallowing back a lump in her throat. *Dear God, please take mercy on this child and answer his prayers. Please make Denny Ray healthy again,* she asked in a silent rush of words.

Denny Ray finally raised his head and blinked his eyes. He looked refreshed, she thought. As if he'd just woken up from a quick restful nap. "Feel any better?" she asked.

He nodded, turning toward her with a look of surprise. "Yeah…I do. I don't feel so scared anymore."

"Good." Ketura reached out and patted his hand. "God is always there for you, Denny Ray. Even when you feel as if you're the only person in the world. He's still there. Watching over you. Listening to your prayers. Will you remember that?"

"I'll try," he promised. He smiled at her, wriggling to sit up a bit higher in the bed against his pile of pillows. "I think I feel like playing checkers now…if you're ready to get beat, that is."

Ketura smiled back broadly. "*Me*? Get beat by *you*? Wait a second, pal. You've got that *all* turned around."

Denny Ray eagerly reached for the box of checkers on his nightstand. "Actions speak louder than words," he said in a very adult tone.

Ketura laughed. "How true… Don't ever forget it, either, Denny Ray."

That night Ketura went to church to hear a special speaker. As he began she leaned forward anxiously for she had waited for weeks for this day. The speaker was Reverend Charles Dewitt, a tall, well-built man with deeply tanned features and prematurely silver hair. He had been preaching for thirty minutes, but it hardly seemed like that to Ket. Reverend Dewitt had been a missionary in India for ten years, and now as he told story after story of how God was working among the very poor, the untouchables as they were called in India, Ket felt her heart swell. She did not take her eyes off the speaker but once and that was when she had to move to let a young boy squeeze by her out of the pew.

As she turned, her glance suddenly fell on a man that was sitting down to her right on the next pew.

She recognized Jared Pierce, and was surprised. Leaning back, she snuck a better view of him. He was listening intently as Reverend Dewitt spoke. Ket could not imagine what he was doing here, because she knew that since he had spoken in church he had not come back. Quickly she looked for Miss Texas, but it appeared that Jared was alone.

Dewitt was coming to the close now and Ket listened, and as he gave the plea for mission volunteers, or for those who had already volunteered, she got up and left her seat. She joined others down at the front, and when Dewitt had gathered them together, he said, "We're going to pray for these. That God will be very rich in their lives. They will all face hard, difficult times, but God will be with you," he said. He passed in front of each one, and when he got in front of Ket, he hesitated. "Are you certain that God has called you to the mission field?"

"Yes, I am, Reverend Dewitt."

"Then He will be with you. Listen for His voice. There's a verse in the Bible that says, 'Thou shall hear a voice behind thee saying this is the way, walk in it.'"

Ket seemed to freeze, for it was the very verse that had echoed in her heart for weeks. Now this was a confirmation!

When she opened the door to her house, Ket could not remember even driving home. Her heart was so full. Her parents were in bed, so she at once showered and put on a gown, but when she lay down she could remember almost every word the speaker had said.

Thank you, Lord, for confirming Your Word. That I will hear a voice. I need to hear Your voice very clearly, for I am unable to find my way without You.

Even as she prayed, something was finding its way into her consciousness. She lay still, for it had become a familiar feeling. She knew that God wanted to convey something to her in the spirit, and for a long time she lay there wide-awake, from time to time praying, *Lord, speak, for thy servant heareth.*

Finally it came, but when it did it sent a shock through her such as she had never received. For the voice said, *I am going to give you a husband, and that husband will be…Jared Pierce.*

Chapter Six

Ket found herself unable to eat breakfast the following morning. She had slept little, for the astonishing and shocking message that she had received from God had turned her world upside down. Not wanting to talk to her parents and let them see that she was agitated, she had left a note on the kitchen counter saying, "Leaving early. See you later. Love, Ket." Bedford whined to go with her, but she just tousled his fur and said, "Not this time, Bedford."

Since it was too early to go to the hospital, she drove into the parking lot and then went out to the fountain. It was a huge affair in a glittering pond, spouting water thirty feet into the air. As she sat down, she watched as the huge colorful carp came to her at once. The fish were accustomed to finding bits of bread tossed into the water.

"Nothing for you today," Ket murmured. She admired the brilliant scarlet colors, redder than anything in nature, and then a gigantic carp with mottled purple and red markings floated by, his filmy fins like lace shimmering in the water.

It was a soothing place where she often came to sit and think or even pray when she had a spare moment, but now she found herself unable to do more than sit there numbly. Finally she got up, heaved a sigh and, glancing at her watch, muttered, "Well, I've got to go to work. What I'd really like to do is go to India."

The day passed quickly and Ket was able to conceal her agitation from the patients very well. One bad moment came, however, when she was sitting at the nurses' station filling out forms. She looked up to see Jared and Dr. Bjelland approaching. She ducked her head, but they stopped not five feet away from her and she could hear their voices plainly as they discussed a patient. She looked up surreptitiously, focussing on his face. She had kept the image of him at church when she saw his profile, but now his face was turned toward her and she studied his features—a strong jaw, lean cheeks and the light blue eyes that could be very direct. He was not looking at her but reading a chart that Dr. Bjelland held out. He had a small scar on his right cheek and she wondered where he had gotten it. Her mind went back to the days when she had seen him play baseball. She remembered watching him play shortstop and how he fielded a bounding grounder, moving smoothly with no sign of urgency. Intercepting the ball in a twisted position he had continued his turn and fired the ball all the way across the diamond to catch the runner at first. It was the sort of grace and strength and agility that only the great ones have. Now she saw that he was still lean and trim.

He's got everything, Ket thought moodily. *He's handsome, and has a beautiful girlfriend who will probably be Miss America. He's a fine doctor. Why would he be interested in me, Lord?* She received no answer and soon the two men moved away.

"I saw you looking over Mr. Hollywood."

Quickly Ket turned to see Debbie Smith standing beside her, an impish light in her gray eyes. Her lips turned upward in a laugh, and she said, "It's hard to keep from looking at *him.*"

"I was just remembering something that happened when we were in high school, that's all." She wasn't lying either, Ket told herself. In truth Ket had been admiring the good looks of Dr. Jared Pierce. Without waiting for Debbie's reply Ket walked away.

Ket tried to brush off Debbie's remark, but it had unsettled her and finally brought her to a decision. She was confused about her own emotions, for she knew that, no matter what she said in her mind or to her friends, she was attracted to Jared. She had argued with herself that he was just another doctor, but she knew deep down that this was not the truth. She tried to shove the remark out of her mind as she went to visit Denny Ray and found that his father was there. "I'm glad to see you, Mr. Kelland. And I bet this boy of yours is, too."

Bill Kelland's skin was burned coppery from the sun. He was in his midforties and he was unable to conceal the worry in his light blue eyes. "I wish I didn't have to leave, but I've got to make a living." He turned to Denny Ray and said, "Hey, champ, I'll be coming back next Friday. Maybe even sooner. Trying to take a whole week off."

"That'd be great, Dad."

Bill Kelland sat on the edge of the bed and took Denny Ray in his arms. Ketura saw the tears in his eyes and in Denny Ray's eyes, too, though the boy forced a bright smile.

"So long, son. I'll be back soon."

Ketura wondered if next week would be soon enough; Denny Ray's condition was so fragile, so precarious. But she didn't want to think the worst. Feeling close to tears herself, she quickly left the room.

Mrs. Kelland followed her. "We appreciate your extra visits so much. I know you don't get paid for that."

"Denny Ray's a special friend of mine. I love to sit with him."

"I'm so worried," Mrs. Kelland said. She had a damp and twisted handkerchief in her hand, and now she pulled at it even more nervously. "He's got a birthday coming up next Thursday. Not a very pleasant place for a young man to have a birthday party."

"Is there going to be a party?" Ket asked quickly.

"Oh, no. He's not up to that."

Ket did not respond, but she made up her mind that there would be a party if she had anything to say about it. Even if she was the only guest.

The next day she went shopping and bought several presents for Denny Ray, one in particular that she'd had on her mind for some time. Then she went directly to the church where she had arranged to meet with the pastor. Pastor Arlen's secretary smiled at her, for she knew Ket well. "Go right in. The pastor's waiting for you."

"Thank you, Maureen."

Once she was inside, Pastor Arlen greeted her warmly. "How's my best mission volunteer today, Ketura?"

"I'm fine, Pastor Arlen."

William Arlen was a very discerning man. He took her answer then leaned back in his chair after she had sat down. "Not too fine though. That's what we all say when someone asks us how we are. Oh, I'm fine. But we're not really."

Ket smiled suddenly. "What would you have someone do when someone says, 'How are you?' Would you have them say, 'Well, sit down. I'll make you out a list of all my woes.'?"

"They'd be bored to death, wouldn't they?" The pastor was a short man, well built, and wore a pair of casual light blue slacks and a white shirt with a maroon tie. "However, this is a little different. People don't ask for appointments because they've come to tell me how good my sermon was."

"You always preach good sermons," Ket said.

"Well, I'm glad you think so." He leaned forward and studied her for a moment. "Something troubling you, Ket?"

"Pastor, does God ever speak to you?"

Arlen blinked with surprise. "Well, that's coming right out with it. Do you mean *audibly?*"

"I mean—in *any* way?"

"Never audibly. I don't think that happens a great deal, although God could certainly speak that way if He chose. He did to Moses."

"But I mean today. Right now. Surely you must have had doubts about what to do? Even preachers must struggle with that."

"Perhaps more than anybody. You want to be more specific? As for me, I try to find answers from Scripture. I pray, and I wait on God. There's no secret to it, Ketura. God has a way of putting things in our hearts. Sometimes it takes a long time. Sometimes we get off on the wrong track."

"Did you ever make a mistake?"

Pastor Arlen threw up his hands. "Make a mistake? Why, certainly! Everybody makes mistakes."

Taking a deep breath, Ket said, "I'm very troubled. Some time ago I began feeling a certain message was coming to me from God…." She told the story quickly and ended by saying, "And so I don't know whether this thing God wants me to do is from Him—or whether it's just my own idea."

"Is it something you've wanted to do for a long time?" Arlen inquired gently.

"No, I never even *thought* of it!"

"Well, that's one good sign. I've known some people who wanted to do something for God, and they talked themselves into the notion of believing that God was telling them to do it. Sometimes He does, sometimes He doesn't."

The two sat there talking for a long time, discussing Ket's situation. Finally the pastor said gently, "They don't teach things like this in the seminary—not exactly. I think all Christians go through times like this, and all I can say is go until you get a caution light. That's what an old friend of mine told me. 'Go until you get a yellow light. Something that says don't go any further, and then wait on God. If you don't get a red light, go until you do get one.'"

Ket smiled ruefully. "That's about what I've been doing, Pastor." She rose, and said, "Thanks very much." He came around the desk then and prayed for her quickly, and as she left the office she said under her breath, "He's such a fine man, but if he knew what I was thinking, he'd probably send me straight to a psychiatrist."

"Happy Birthday!"

Denny Ray looked up with surprise as Ket entered his room. She had a small cake with eleven candles burning brightly in one hand, a bunch of balloons tied to her wrist and two brightly wrapped packages in the other. "If you blow them all out in one breath, you get a wish. So think of something good."

Denny Ray was propped up with pillows behind him. His face was pale and looked small and defensive. But his eyes lit up, and he inflated his lungs and blew out.

"There, I did it!"

"What did you wish?"

"You can't tell," he announced, "or it won't come true."

"That's right. Here. You open your presents and I'll cut the cake."

Denny Ray looked at the packages. "I hate to mess up this pretty wrapping."

"It's all right. That's what it's for." Ket tied the balloons to a rail at the foot of his bed and started to slice the cake.

Both of her gifts were roughly the same size and shape. Ketura could see it was hard to choose which one to open first. Finally he grabbed the package on the right and tore off the wrapping.

She watched his face, wondering what his reaction would be.

"Gee…a Bible." He seemed surprised but not displeased, she thought. "I don't have one of these. That's for sure."

Ketura laughed. "It's a children's edition. There are lots of cool pictures, and the stories are written in a way that's easy to understand."

Denny Ray shrugged, leafing quickly through the pages. "I like stories."

"Yes, I know you do. We can read it together sometime if you want to."

He looked pleased by that idea, she thought. "Sure…maybe later. Can I open the other one now?"

"Absolutely," Ketura replied. He quickly opened the next gift and let out a whoop of pleasure. "Wow, Ket! This is great! Super Sam…I didn't know there were videos."

He looked up at her, his face glowing with gratitude and wonder.

"They just came out. I know you like the books, so I thought the videos would be fun. I think there are a few new stories there, so it won't be totally boring for you."

"Super Sam could never be boring! Want to watch one with me?"

"Sure, let's put one on while we have our cake."

"Okay," Denny Ray sat up in bed, looking bright-eyed and eager for the show to begin.

Ketura turned on the video player below the TV and put in a video. Soon the theme music began, and she could sense Denny Ray's excitement. It hadn't taken much on her part to observe that Super Sam—a crime-fighting, mystery-solving basset hound—was his favorite book character. He seemed to read little else. When she spotted the videos in the store, she knew they would please him, though she'd never guessed how much. Denny Ray sat smiling, totally immersed in the hound's latest escapades, and Ketura felt satisfied. She'd wanted so much to give him a special gift, one that would take his mind off his illness for a while.

She cut the cake and slipped the slices onto paper plates, then served Denny Ray a slice along with a paper cup of cola. Then she cut herself a slice and sat down next to him.

Denny Ray eagerly took the cake and ate a bite. "This is good!" he said. "Where did you get it?"

"I made it. What do you think—I'd give my friend a store-bought cake for his birthday?"

"You really did?"

"I really did. I hope you like chocolate," she teased him.

"Ket—you know that's my favorite!"

Denny Ray sat there and was soon lost in the story. Ket was glad to see him so entertained and able to forget his illness for a while. She sat quietly beside him, watching his face mostly.

When the movie was over, she asked, "Did you like it?"

"It was super! Can we watch another one?"

"No, not right now. I think you need to rest. I'll put your cake right here. I've wrapped it up so that it'll stay fresh. Maybe your mother would like some."

"She's coming in later."

Ket went over and leaned over and kissed his cheek. "Happy birthday, Denny Ray," she whispered.

"Thanks!" He looked up at her and then tilted his head to one side. "Do you really think I'm going to get well? I—I don't think the doctors believe that."

"I'm praying for you every day, and I'm believing that God will help you grow up to be a big, strong man. Who knows, maybe you'll be a pastor or an evangelist."

"Or maybe a ballplayer."

Ket laughed and tousled his hair. "Maybe even that! I'll come back when I'm off-duty."

She left the room and as she went about her duties, she thought often of Denny Ray's question. *Lord,* she prayed, *all things are in Your hands. But You know how much I love this boy. Not as much as You do, but a lot. So I'm asking You to work a miracle in his life.*

Jared Pierce didn't know why he kept returning to the church where he had spoken. Lisa had not volunteered to go back, but there had been a spirit in the congregation, and something in the pastor that drew him back—something he found missing in his life. He reasoned out that the pastor was witty and at the same time a highly spiritual man, but he knew that it was more than that. Jared felt an impression of love among he congregation, which seemed to him to be a very rare thing indeed.

On Sunday morning he was sitting in the pew and Pastor Arlen was preaching when suddenly Jared heard him quoting from Scripture and felt an electrifying sensation along his spine. "When shall it profit a man if he gained the whole world and lose his own soul?" the minister was quoting.

Jared had heard evangelists and pastors talk about

how a certain Scripture could suddenly strike an individual so deeply, it penetrated right to his heart. That was exactly the way it happened with him. He did not hear much of the rest of the sermon, for the verse kept pounding over and over in his mind like a song that someone can not quit singing. *"What shall it profit a man.... What shall it profit a man.... What shall it profit a man…?"*

He suddenly became aware that his hands were sweating and felt unsteady. Taking out his handkerchief he wiped his palms, glancing around to see if anyone was watching, and then he heard the pastor say, "We will now give you an opportunity to make your profession of faith in Jesus Christ. Some of you here may have already decided 'It doesn't profit me none of this world's possessions if I don't have Jesus.' Won't you come down this aisle and we will pray together, and then you will find the true riches that are in God."

Standing there through that hymn was one of the most difficult experiences of Jared's life. He was being torn in two, for part of him wanted to go forward and pray, and to be prayed for, for he knew suddenly that his life was barren and empty despite all the trappings of success.

Still, there was another force that would not let him take a step. It was as though his feet were set in cement. He gripped the back of the pew in front of him with both hands and kept his head down staring at them as the hymn went on. They were singing, *"Just as I am without one plea, but that Thy blood was shed for me.'"*

And somehow this riveted him. He knew that he was a Christian and that he was saved, for he had been converted when he was a very young man, but he could not escape from something that was happening inside of him.

As he turned to leave, with some relief he thought, *Something is wrong in my life. I've got to find out what it is.*

On his way out, Pastor Arlen stood there and offered his hand, saying, "Good to see you again, Jared. How have you been?"

"All right, I suppose." Jared shrugged. "Just trying to sort out a few things," he admitted.

Pastor Arlen nodded. "It's sometimes a struggle to find what God wants us to do, but I'm sure, my brother, that if you continue, you'll find what God has for you."

Startled by the pastor's insight, Pierce murmured, "Thanks a lot," and then left the church more disturbed than he had been in years.

Jared had not seen Ketura in church but she had caught sight of him as he'd entered, and from time to time during the sermon had watched him. It was the second time she had the opportunity to observe him while she herself remained relatively invisible. She noticed his intent expression and the troubled look on his face as he sat staring down at the floor, lost in his own thoughts. Hardly the confident, self-possessed doctor she knew from Mercy Hospital. She sensed he was going through some kind of a struggle and wondered at it. She did not attempt to speak to Jared but watched as he left.

When she shook hands with the pastor, he said, "Still waiting for a red light?"

"Yes, I am."

"It may never come. God bless you, Ketura."

Ket left the church thinking how disturbed she had been over the Word that kept coming to her. *You will marry Jared Pierce.* Doubts had come along with that and now as she walked slowly toward her car, she prayed, *"Lord, I'm being torn in two by all of this. Please make Your will clear to me!"*

Chapter Seven

Looking up at the sign in front of her, Ket felt a spasm of irritation. It was on her regular route to work and she'd seen it many times before. It simply said Koffee Shop. Yet for some reason it annoyed her.

"You'd think anybody would know how to spell coffee with a *c* instead of a *k!*"

She'd no sooner said the words aloud than she spotted another sign that said Dave's Dri-Kleener, which made her feel even more irrate.

She knew it was irrational. She certainly had better things to think about, and why worry about these silly signs today? Hadn't she seen them hundreds of time before? But even as she forced her thoughts in a new direction, she spotted yet another and even more outrageous example. X-Eye Ting Optiks.

"X-Eye Ting Optiks." Ket shook her head. "Isn't that cute? I ought to give up nursing and start a crusade for real spelling."

She pulled into the hospital parking lot, relieved to see signs with real words and standard spellings. She strode toward the entrance taking deep, calming breaths and trying to settle her nerves. She knew it wasn't the cute spelling on store signs making her so jumpy today. It was her problem with Jared Pierce.

As she entered the hospital she found herself watching nervously for him. They hadn't really spoken since the time she'd assisted him in the E.R. Since then, they had passed in the hallways a few times, but he'd barely acknowledged her with a quick nod. Ketura didn't have all that much experience with men, but even she knew this was not the way a man acted who was interested and attracted.

She worried about herself. Was she imagining…everything? She'd heard of stalkers and people who conjured up elaborate emotional connections that were all in their own mind, but she was always so logical about such matters. Too logical, maybe. She couldn't imagine herself in that category. The whole situation was so unnerving. She didn't want to be so distracted and upset that she would make a mistake in her work. She could ruin her chance to become an R.N. Or worse yet, unintentionally harm a patient.

Now, as she headed down the hallway toward Denny Ray's room, she silently scolded herself. *You've just got to stop it, Ket. If God's in it, you'll be all right.*

Then, immediately the thought came, *But what if He's not in it?*

Ignoring the worry, she turned into the room and

saw Mr. and Mrs. Kelland, one on each side of Denny Ray's bed. "Hi," she said cheerfully. "I just stopped in to say hello. But no time for checkers this morning, sorry."

"I don't feel much like it anyway," Denny Ray said weakly. His eyes were droopy and his color was as pale as paste.

Ket went over and tweaked his toes. "You get a little rest. I'll come back when you feel better." Turning, she left the room but she had not gone far before she heard her name.

"Nurse!" She turned to see Bill Kelland standing there, an anxious light in his eyes. "I keep forgetting your name. Is it Lindsey?"

"That's right. Ketura Lindsey." Bill Kelland chewed his lower lip and shifted his weight uncertainly. "I never thought I'd be in anything like this," he admitted. "Me and Ellen had given up on having a kid, and then suddenly Denny Ray was born. I mean it was like winning the lottery a hundred times over, only better. I'd always wanted a boy. Someone to play ball with, and Ellen she had always just wanted a baby. She's got a real mother instinct."

"He's a fine boy, Mr. Kelland."

"Yeah, he is. No trouble at all. Not like some of these kids making their parents crazy." Bill Kelland pulled out a package of cigarettes and pulled one out. He started to put it to his lips, then blinked. "What am I doing?" he mumbled. "Can't smoke in here. Need to quit anyway." He shoved the package back into his pocket and then clenched his fists and slapped them against his sides with an odd mannerism. It was as if he wanted to strike out at someone, but who was the enemy? Who could he hit?

Ket knew that many relatives and friends of very sick people felt the same way. Gently, she said, "I'm praying that he'll be all right."

Quickly his eyes focused on her. He swallowed hard and shook his head. "I guess I ain't much for religion. Ellen takes Denny Ray to church from time to time. But me, I never go." He paused and sighed, looking past her. "I used to go when I was a kid. With my grandmother, she was a great woman. She used to read the Bible to me, too. Haven't thought about that in a long time. Took me to church, sat with me. I must have been a pest, but she never got after me, you know?"

Ketura didn't know how to respond, but knew she didn't really have to say anything. Bill Kelland simply needed someone to listen right now. She was in the middle of a busy workday and had so many places to be, so many duties to perform, but she knew it was important now to stand right here and hear him out. That was part of being a good nurse, too, she thought. Even if she found herself scolded by some supervisor later.

"You must have loved your grandmother very much," she said finally.

"Yes, I did. But I didn't appreciate her until after she was gone." He shook his head. "Isn't that always the way?" He met her glance a moment, and she knew he was thinking about Denny Ray.

"Denny Ray told me what you did for his birthday…and how you said a prayer with him when he felt scared," he added quietly. "I guess I just wanted you to know that Ellen and me, we really appreciate it. It helps to know that someone like you is looking after him. Especially when we can't be here."

Ketura smiled shyly. "Denny Ray's sort of a special friend of mine."

"Well, he's a lucky boy to have found a friend like you. If you ask me, this hospital is awful lucky to have you, too."

His sincere compliments made her feel self-conscious but proud.

"I know nurses and doctors do all they can, but sometimes I think it's going to take more than medicine to help my son…. Do you know what I mean?" he asked quietly.

"Yes…I do, Mr. Kelland. But nothing is impossible for God."

Bill Kelland looked surprised for a moment by her reply. "That's what my grandmother used to tell me."

"Well…she was right," Ketura replied.

He didn't answer right away. "Maybe so," he said finally.

"Dad? Are you still out there?" They both turned at the sound of Denny Ray's voice.

His father stepped forward and poked his head inside the room. "I'm still here, son. Just talking to Nurse Lindsey."

"She's the greatest," Ketura heard Denny Ray answer. "If everybody was like her, it'd be a pretty good world, huh, Dad?"

"Pretty good world," Bill Kelland replied. Then he glanced back at Ketura and smiled. "Yes, indeed. A pretty good world."

When Bill Kelland met her gaze with his grateful smile, she felt awkward again. But she also felt a sense of quiet satisfaction, knowing she was a source of comfort and support for Denny Ray and his family during this difficult time.

Jared walked into his apartment and closed the door. He tossed his keys and some mail on the table and slung his jacket over an armchair. The place looked messy and out of control, but as usual, he felt too weary to tackle a cleanup. His apartment was only a pit stop lately. He barely had time to eat, shower and sleep here on his way back and forth from the hospital. Home a bit earlier tonight, he longed for a hot shower and night of mindless relaxation, watching baseball on TV.

He picked up a huge pile of old newspapers and began to sort through them. Then the phone rang, distracting him. He let the answering machine pick up, but when he heard Lisa's voice on the line, he felt a sudden shock.

I had a date with Lisa tonight! I forgot all about it! He quickly checked his watch. Half past six. *If I take a fast shower I can still pick her up by seven-thirty. I won't be too late.* They could simply go out to dinner some place…and talk.

Then he felt a stab of dread. He had to have a serious talk with Lisa about their relationship. He couldn't put it off any longer. They wanted different things from life, they clearly had different values. His feelings for her had changed and he'd finally faced it. He sensed that she had her doubts about him lately, too. It didn't take much for her to start a fight these days. Maybe if they talked openly, they could finally clear the air. It wouldn't be easy, but he knew it was the right thing to do.

Lisa had been talking into the answering machine, leaving a long message, but Jared hadn't heard a word of it. He ran over to the phone and snatched up the receiver.

"Lisa—I'm glad you called. I'm running a little late…."

"That's okay. Didn't you hear my message? I'm really sorry, but I can't make it tonight, Jared. Something's come up. It's very exciting actually. I had a call from a big Hollywood agent today. I've been in touch with him a few times, sent my photos and such. He's in town and wants to meet with me. He might take me on as a client. Isn't that exciting?"

Jared sat down in a kitchen chair. It sounded like Lisa was breaking their date. He was surprised. But in another way, not surprised at all.

"Yes…very exciting," he agreed.

"He's going back to Los Angeles tonight on a late

flight, and he said the only time he had available was this evening. I couldn't say no. Who knows? This could be the chance of a lifetime."

"It could be," he agreed.

"You know, I always thought I'd have to win the pageant in order to get a chance at the movies or TV. But maybe that doesn't even matter. Maybe I'll get there anyway. Some things are just fate, you know?"

Fate? He didn't believe in that. He believed in God's plan, but didn't think Lisa was talking about quite the same thing. That was just the problem. They were never talking about the same thing anymore.

"What's the matter, Jared? You don't sound happy for me." Her tone was hurt and accusatory. "Are you jealous or something? It's just a business meeting, for goodness' sake."

"Jealous? Not at all," he said honestly. But the reply seemed to make her even madder.

"Well, you sound like you must be. Why don't you say something positive? You know that I've always dreamed of being in the movies or in television."

"I *am* happy for you. Really. I mean, if this is what you really want, Lisa. But acting is a hard life. I'm not sure you realize how hard. It's like being in a beauty contest every day."

"I'm not afraid of that," she said confidently. "I'm not afraid one bit. I'll need to move to California, of course…. But there are sick people there, too, I've heard," she teased.

"True enough. But I've never thought of moving to California," he added honestly.

He heard only silence on the other end of the phone, and he thought for a moment Lisa had hung up.

"Well…maybe you ought to start thinking about it. That's the problem with you, Jared. You're so wrapped up in that hospital. You're like a turtle in a shell. You need to poke your head out once in a while and check out the real world."

The real world? Did she mean competing in beauty pageants?

It didn't get any *realer* than the emergency room at Mercy Hospital, as far as he could see. He felt his heart beat quicken, but he checked his anger. This wasn't the time for an argument. There really was no argument. It just didn't work between them anymore. That was crystal clear. But he had been involved with Lisa for a long time, and he knew that whatever impasse they now faced was not entirely her doing.

"Lisa, I'm sorry you feel that way. I think we need to get together soon, to talk about our relationship. Our future." He tried hard to express his thoughts in a way that didn't sound like blaming or fault-finding. "I know I've been busy with school and now my internship. And you've been so busy with the pageant. But I feel that for a long time we've been moving in different directions…."

Lisa let out a long, exasperated sigh. "Yes, Jared…I know what you mean. We've both been really busy lately… But I really can't get into it now. I have to get ready for my meeting. I'm not even sure what to wear," she said anxiously. "Maybe we can talk tomorrow night or something…okay?"

"I'm at the hospital the next two nights. But I get off early on Friday. How about dinner?"

"Friday night sounds fine. Well…wish me luck." Her voice was bright with anticipation, Jared thought. Looking ahead to sunny California and the stardom she believed awaited her there. She wasn't exactly torn to pieces about their differences, was she?

"Good luck, Lisa. I hope it goes well for you. I feel certain it will," he said sincerely. His tone was bittersweet. But he didn't think she noticed.

"Thanks a lot. You're sweet. I'll let you know the outcome," she promised.

Then she said goodbye and quickly hung up. He sat gazing at the phone for a moment, feeling surprised by her brisk close to their conversation. Either she really didn't care if they stopped seeing each other or she was a better actress than he'd ever imagined.

He felt sad but also relieved to have finally voiced his doubts. At least he'd been honest with her. They would talk more on Friday. It wouldn't be easy, but in a way he looked forward to getting his feelings out in the open.

How would her meeting with the agent go? She'd do well, he guessed. Very well. When the spotlight was on, Lisa knew how to shine, how to turn on the charm and show her beauty to full advantage. She knew what she wanted and how to go after it—he'd say that for her. Though it seemed that being a doctor's wife had dropped to the bottom of her wish list. Or maybe been scratched off entirely...

He walked into his small living room and flicked on the TV. The station was already tuned to the ball game, which was just about to start. He watched the pitcher warming up, but instead of thinking about the home team's prospects tonight, or even about Lisa, he kept hearing instead the words of the sermon he'd listened to the previous Sunday. *"What shall it profit a man if he gained the whole world and lose his own soul?"*

"Why do I keep thinking of that?" he grumbled. "I'm a Christian. How am I going to lose my soul?" With a feeling that edged on bafflement and even irritation, he began to pray aloud. "God, I wish You'd either take this verse out of my head or else let me know what it's about. Because I sure don't have any idea!"

"Wow, that was a good one." Denny Ray took his eyes off the television set and smiled. "I really like these videos you gave me, Ket."

"You must. I think you've memorized all of them."

As usual Ketura had stopped by to say good-night to Denny Ray and had found him watching one of the videos she had given him for his birthday. She had sat beside him, amused that he could move his lips in sync with the characters on the screen.

Denny Ray seemed better tonight. His eyes were brighter and he was more alert. Ket smoothed his bedding and shook out his pillows.

"What's it like to be a nurse?"

"What's it like? What do you mean, Denny Ray?"

"I mean it must be cool being able to make sick people well."

"Well, when I can help somebody, it gives me a real good feeling."

"You've helped me a lot," the boy told her.

"I haven't done much, but I'm going to do more."

"Tell me some more about the doctors in the old days."

To her surprise Ket had discovered that Denny Ray was very interested in history. She had accidentally mentioned some obscure fact about the early days of medicine, and almost inevitably he would ask for details.

"Well, one thing you must remember is that most disease is caused by germs. Germs are like tiny insects, so small you can only see them with a microscope. Germs thrive in dark, dirty places. Years ago nobody knew that. Millions of people must have died just for that reason."

"You mean they didn't take baths?"

"For the most part no. In the first place it was very hard to take a bath. People could bathe in water outdoors, like a lake, or a river, or stream. But only in warm weather. There wasn't any indoor plumbing or running water. Most people lived in a one-room hut or cottage. A lucky few lived in a castle, which was a cold place of stone and had no way to heat water except over an open fire. The servants could do it, of course," Ket said, "but nobody really cared that much about bathing."

"They must have smelled real bad."

Ket laughed. "I imagine they did."

"But everybody smelled bad so they probably didn't notice it."

"Probably not. You or I would probably keel over if we walked into a wealthy home back in the medieval days. The people would have been handsome and courteous, but you would have seen what you would call weeds strewn on the dining room floor. There wouldn't be many plates, and for the most part the food was served on slices of bread and eaten with the fingers. Anything you didn't want you threw on the floor to be eaten by the dogs, or the cats, or to rot there."

"Yuck!" Denny Ray frowned. "Sounds awful!"

Ket smiled fondly at a memory that came to her. "I once loved movies about the Middle Ages. The beautiful ladies wearing their beautiful gowns, the gentlemen wearing even more beautiful clothes sometimes, but then one day when I read about a ball that Queen Elizabeth I gave for the Duke of Essex, it told about all that and then I thought, none of those people at the party had bathed in probably six months or more. Can you imagine that?" Ketura made a face and pinched her nose with her forefinger and thumb. "Not very elegant!"

Denny Ray laughed. "Pretty yucky party. For a queen, I mean. Tell me more, Ketura. Please?"

"Yes…tell us more," a deep voice in the doorway echoed.

Ketura quickly turned to find Jared standing in the doorway. His amused expression suggested he'd been standing there a while, listening to her conversation with Denny Ray. She felt her cheeks flush and was thankful for the room's low light.

She quickly turned toward Denny Ray's bed. "Not tonight. It's getting late. You need to get some rest," she said to the boy.

Jared stood at the foot of the bed, watching her. "Dr. Bjelland asked me to do his round tonight," he explained to Ketura, though she had already guessed as much. She nodded, but didn't reply, busying herself with tasks around the bedside. She saw her hand shake as she poured Denny Ray a fresh cup of water and she had an impulse to dash out of the room. Then she realized she didn't want to leave Denny Ray so abruptly and also was curious to see if there would be any sign at all from Jared that the message she'd had about him was true.

Jared picked up the medical chart and looked over the information. Then he sat at the edge of the bed, took out his stethoscope and listened to Denny Ray's heart.

"Hi, Denny Ray. How are you feeling?" he asked kindly.

"Not so bad." The boy shrugged. "I'd feel a lot better if Nurse Lindsey would stick around and tell me some more stories. I know it's late. But my dad says she's good medicine for me."

Jared smiled at Ket and she smiled back, despite the butterflies churning in her stomach.

"I can see that," he agreed. "If we could figure out some way to bottle what Nurse Lindsey has going for her…well, the doctors around here might be out of business."

Denny Ray laughed. "Wouldn't that be something?"

Ketura shook her head. "Wouldn't it, though?"

Jared laughed at her. He examined Denny Ray a bit more, then stood up and ruffled the boy's hair with his hand. "It *is* late. You ought to get some sleep."

Denny Ray turned to Ketura, who stood on the other side of the bed. "Will you tuck me in and say a prayer?" he asked her.

That had become their usual routine when she visited at night and Denny Ray's mother wasn't there. "Of course," she said. "Scoot under the covers."

As Denny Ray settled into bed, Ketura expected Jared to leave and continue with his rounds. But instead, he stood by quietly watching.

"Okay, let's say a prayer now," Denny Ray said. Ketura bowed her head and so did Jared while Denny Ray said The Lord's Prayer aloud. Then Denny Ray spoke aloud to God, praying in his own way.

"…and please watch over my folks and help them be less worried about me. And please keep helping me get better, God. I do feel a little better every day…. Amen."

"Amen," Ketura said.

"Amen," Jared added in his deep voice.

Ketura met his gaze for a moment. His expression was serious and thoughtful. But impossible to fathom.

Concern for Denny Ray, she decided. Nothing that had to do with her.

Denny Ray sank back against the pillow, and she kissed his forehead. Jared shut off the bedside light as the boy murmured, "Good night, Ketura. Good night, Dr. Pierce…"

"Good night, tiger. See you tomorrow," Jared promised.

Out in the brightly lit corridor, Ketura felt suddenly awkward and shy. She walked purposely down the hall and soon realized Jared had fallen in step beside her.

"You've done a lot for Denny Ray. You *are* good medicine for him. The best kind."

Ketura shrugged. "I'm just trying to do my job, to be a good nurse. Denny Ray is a very special boy. I always feel as if I can't do enough for him. Or maybe more like nothing anyone can do will be enough…. Do you know what I mean?"

She met Jared's gaze a moment and he nodded. "I understand."

Ketura paused. She needed to stand back and be objective. Observe how Jared acted around her. Now she'd gotten carried away in her concern about Denny Ray. She took a breath and gathered her thoughts.

"How is he doing? He says he feels better. Is that possible?"

Jared didn't answer at first. "Anything's possible. He doesn't appear to be getting any worse. So that's some encouragement."

"Yes, some." She looked up at him, waiting for him to say more.

"Dr. Bjelland is doing all he can. We all are…. I guess it's up to God now," Jared said quietly. "Prayers might help," he added.

"I do pray for him," Ketura replied.

"Yes, I'm sure you do…. So do I," he confided. He glanced at her and seemed about to say more. Then the pager in the pocket of his white coat sounded. He fished it out and checked the number.

"Got to run. See you around."

"Sure. See you." Ketura watched him turn the corner at the end of the hallway and head toward the elevators.

Ketura had already finished her shift. She picked up her belongings and headed out to the parking lot. On the drive home, she reviewed her conversation with Jared—every word, every look.

He was different from the way she remembered him. More thoughtful. More compassionate. She'd noticed that while working with him in the E.R., too. Maybe those traits had come with some maturity and from studying medicine. Or perhaps from losing his chance to play professional baseball and having to cope with that challenge. Maybe he'd always been that way, but she'd only known him from a distance.

Still, he'd shown her nothing tonight to confirm the messages she'd heard. He'd been polite and friendly. His praise for the way she cared for Denny Ray had been generous and made her feel good about her work.

But it was still all on a professional level. He'd shown no interest in her in any other way—certainly not in a romantic way.

Ketura felt frustrated and deflated. She'd hoped that if she had the chance to see him again and talk privately, some small sign would be revealed. But now that she had seen him, she felt more confused than ever.

At home, the evening passed quickly. She watched television with her mother, and after, took time out to romp with Bedford. Her favorite ball team was playing, and she loyally sat through every inning, though they were getting soundly trounced.

"I don't know why they can't win every game," her father complained when the game ended.

"It wouldn't be any fun then, Dad," Ket said. She went over and kissed him, then did the same to her mother. "Good night. I'll see you in the morning."

Up in her room, she closed the door and took out her journal. She sat in the window seat and noted her meeting with Jared and how he had acted around her.

He's polite and professional toward me. Even complimentary at times. Friendly, too, I'd guess you could say. But he hardly seems to notice me as more than a colleague. Certainly not as a woman he'd consider to be his future wife.

When she had finished, she looked back over the pages and found the entry that recorded the first time she had felt God telling her she was going to be married. Turning the pages, she followed the progression of her experience, but finally closed the book abruptly. She sat holding the diary in her lap and sighed. "This voice behind me... I sure wish someone else could hear it."

She went over to the window and looked out, and waited, as if she expected God to speak to her more clearly than he had so far. When nothing came, she shrugged and prepared for bed. She did not go to bed, however, but sat down on the window seat again and pulled the reading light closer. She felt tired and discouraged and just held the Bible in her hand, not even praying for a while. Finally she said aloud, "Lord, You want me to be honest with You. You know what's in my heart. I'm discouraged and I'm tired, and to tell the truth I don't think any of this makes any sense. Why would Jared Pierce marry me? He hardly knows I'm alive."

Somehow in the silence that followed, Ket felt very uncomfortable. It was almost as if she had said, *I don't believe You, God.* Of all things, this was not what she wanted, for she was hungry for more of the Lord.

Finally she closed her eyes and began to pray, and somehow the discomfort increased. That which came to her was not really in words—it was more of a feeling. If it had been in words, it would have been something like, *Why do you doubt Me, Ketura? Don't you know that I can do anything?*

"I know you can do anything, Lord, but it's hard to believe that something like this could happen."

And again the whispering impression, *But that's what I do for My people.*

For some reason at that moment Ket had an impulse. The Bible was lying on her lap, and stirred by what had come into her mind, she opened it and began to thumb through the book of Genesis. It was all very familiar to her and she skimmed the pages, waiting for something to catch her attention. She knew God had something to teach her here, and finally, when she came to chapter eighteen, it was as if the voice whispered, *Stop! Read this.*

So she began to read the story of how God appeared to Abraham and promised him that he would have a son. Both Abraham and his wife Sarah were quite old. Sarah was far beyond the age of childbearing, and the idea of creating a child seemed impossible to Abraham. When Sarah heard the same message, the Scripture continued, she couldn't believe it, either, and even laughed. Then, in verse fourteen, Ketura read, "Is anything too hard for the Lord? At the time appointed I will return unto thee, according to the time of life, and Sarah shall have a son."

Ket read the passage twice and slowly felt a new insight into her own predicament come to her. "Sarah laughed, thinking You were not able to give her a son even though she was old, but You did give her a son," she said aloud. "Lord, I've been doubtful, but I'm going to believe Your Word, and I'm going to expect what

You have told me in secret will come to pass. I *am* going to marry Jared Pierce!"

She sat there, her eyes closed, feeling totally calm. Then an impression came again. Not with a voice but as a feeling of something she knew she had to do.

I am pleased with Your faith. Now tell your parents what I have spoken unto you.

Ketura's eyes flew open. She wanted to cry out, "Lord, I can't do it. They'll think I've lost my mind."

Instead her lips moved as she faintly said, "Lord, I will obey no matter how foolish I look."

She got up, went to bed and a peace came upon her so that she immediately fell asleep.

Chapter Eight

Ket sat straight up in her chair. She stared at her parents, and nervously licked her lips. Finally she took a deep breath and tried to smile. "Well," she said, and cleared her throat, "I guess you're wondering why I've called you together."

It was a poor attempt at an opener but it was the best that Ket could do. She had firmly decided to be obedient to what she felt was the voice of the Lord, so immediately after breakfast on Friday morning she had said, "Mom, Dad, I need to talk to you."

"Now?" her father had asked in surprise. "I'm running a little bit late, Ket."

"This won't take long, but there's something I have to say." She did not miss the look of apprehension that had come to both of her parents but forced herself to continue. Vainly trying to postpone the moment of truth, she said, "I know it always sounds ominous when someone says, 'I have to talk to you.'"

"Is it ominous, Ket?" Roger asked gently, concern in his blue eyes.

"Oh, I'm not sick or anything like that! But something's been…well…troubling me for some time."

"You haven't been yourself lately," Lucille said quickly. "Your father and I have both noticed it."

"I don't think there's any way to put this in a way that won't shock you, so I'll just tell it as it is." She leaned forward and clasped her hands together and knew that it was hopeless to try to take the shock out of her words. "About three weeks ago I began to feel that God was telling me to do something. You know how it is when you're not right sure so you wait and then usually it takes shape."

"I've had that happen many times." Roger nodded. "It would be nice if it came all at once in a neat package and we didn't have any question in our minds, but it doesn't usually happen that way, does it?"

"What is it, Ket? Is it about India?"

"No. God has already confirmed that I'm going to India as a medical missionary, but this was something else." She hesitated one moment then shrugged her shoulders. "Well, I have the strongest impression that God was telling me that He was going to give me…a husband."

"Is that all?" Her father exhaled a deep breath and shrugged his shoulders. "I thought it was something dreadful."

"Why, I think that's wonderful, Ket!" Lucille beamed. She had worried a great deal about this younger daughter of hers, concerned that she would never find a loving partner to share her life. It was difficult enough to give her up to India, but she had so longed to see Ket find a good man and get married. Now she smiled and reached over and put her hand on Roger's. "Why, that's wonderful news."

"Well, that's not—not all of it, exactly," Ket stammered a little. "I prayed and prayed about this, and finally the Lord told me something else. This is what you might find to be a problem."

A silence fell across the room and the only sound was the whirring of the neighbor's lawn mower next door—that, and the ticking of the clock on a shelf.

"Well, He's told me that I'm to marry...Jared Pierce."

"Jared Pierce! Why, Ket, he's practically engaged to Lisa!"

Nervously Ket twisted in her chair. She had come to the part that she was most afraid of sharing with her parents, but forged ahead as well as she could. "I've been over all that, Mom. But I still feel that God has told me I'm going to marry him...." She spoke rapidly as she related her experience, and the more she spoke, the more foolish she felt.

"Well, I suppose God does intend for you to marry him." Roger smiled slightly. "What about you? Are you interested in him? From what I recall you never even liked him when you were a child."

Nervously Ket uttered a short laugh. "Every single woman in the hospital is interested in him—and some that aren't single." She spread her hands out with a gesture of hopelessness. "Why, Dad, he's as handsome as a movie star, he comes from a good family and he's dating Miss Texas. Now, let me ask you why in the world he would pay any attention to me?"

Both of her parents stared at her for a moment, and then Lucille said quickly, "Perhaps it was just your own idea."

"That might be, " Ket's father agreed. "Do you have a secret crush on him?"

"Of course not!" Ket snapped at her father. "He's been friendly when we meet at the hospital. But I rarely even see him. I never once thought about dating him. And then I'd just gotten to the part where I could accept God's promise that I would be married when this came up."

"How strong an impression is it, Ket?" Roger asked cautiously. "We do make mistakes. Why, even when you pray and meditate on these questions, a person can make mistakes in things like this."

"I don't know, Dad. I've told God the same thing, but how do you tell God He's made a mistake? If that's what He's saying, that I'm supposed to marry Jared Pierce, I can't tell Him He's wrong, can I?"

"No, you can't do that." Roger sat there quietly for a moment and then shook his head. "Have you told anybody else?"

"I told the pastor part of it. Not using Jared's name, of course."

"What did he say?"

"He said to go until I got a caution light and then a red light. But I haven't gotten that so far."

"Well, I think the pastor's right." Roger nodded. "Keep on praying, and now we'll pray with you."

A rush of gratitude came to Ket. She got up and went over to her parents, who rose at the same time. "I'm such a lot of trouble to you," she murmured.

"Nonsense!" Roger gave her a squeeze and stepped back as her mother kissed her cheek. "You've not been a minute's trouble. We love you, Ket, and want the best for you. I guess we have to wait and see what God does."

On Friday night, Jared drove straight from the hospital to the French restaurant where he had planned to meet Lisa. He felt nervous about confronting her, but knew he had to say what was on his mind. He'd thought about it a lot over the past two days and he just couldn't see any future for them. Not a happy one. He wondered how she would react. Would she scream at him? Or maybe cry? He really didn't want to hurt her. But he knew now that even her tears wouldn't melt his resolve.

He spotted Lisa right away when he entered the restaurant; she was seated at a corner table at the far end of the room. She smiled—her dazzling, pageant-winner smile—and waved. She looked gorgeous as usual, wearing an ice-blue sleeveless dress made of some thin, silky fabric, her golden hair loose around her shoulders. Yet, as he approached and kissed her cheek, he felt distant and unmoved by her beauty. The feeling saddened him and at the same time, sharpened his intentions.

"I've ordered already for you. I hope you don't mind," Lisa said. "Something's come up. Sort of an emergency. I can't stay too long…. Sorry, Jared." She glanced up at him from under her lashes with an apologetic expression.

Jared felt caught off balance. "Everything is okay at home, I hope?"

"Oh, sure. It's nothing like that." Lisa sat back and shook her head. "It's good news, actually. Great news, I'd say. I'm sorry that I didn't get to tell you sooner. But I knew we'd get together tonight. At least for a little while—"

"Tell me what?"

"I'm flying out to Los Angeles tonight! Isn't that fantastic?" Her voice had risen several octaves as she spoke, so that her last words came out almost a shriek of delight. She sat back in her chair, beaming at him.

Jared didn't know what to say. "Well…that's new. What's the rush?"

"Remember that agent I told you about? We met for dinner on Tuesday night?" Jared nodded, recalling their broken date. "Well, he took me on as a client and he spoke to a casting director about me. He's set up an audition for a part in a movie! Isn't that unbelievable?"

"Yes…it is," Jared replied honestly. "So, you're going out to California tonight for the audition?"

Lisa nodded. She picked up a piece of bread, stared at it, then put it down again.

"Well, there's that and then some other appointments during the week. My agent said since I'm out there, I might as well make the most of the trip. He's going to take me around, have me meet people. Go to parties, that sort of thing." She paused and glanced at Jared, as if testing his reaction, he thought.

"Sounds exciting," he said.

Lisa laughed at him. "I'll say it's exciting. It's unbelievable. It's fantastic. It's the best thing that's ever happened in my life. That's *all.* You always did have a flair for understatement, Jared."

The waiter had brought the salad course and Jared speared a leafy bite with his fork. He didn't know how to reply.

Lisa took a breath and sipped her water. She stared at him and Jared sensed there was something more she wanted to say. "The thing is," she began, "my agent told me I may be out there for a while. Not just a week or two. A long time, I mean. One thing leads to another, you know. Or at least, I hope it will. If I get the part in this movie and other jobs, I'll need to move out there…permanently."

"Yes, that's probably true." He glanced at her. "How do you feel about that?"

She shrugged. "I love California. And you know how much I'd love to be in the movies…. But I've thought about this a lot, Jared, and I know you don't want to move there. You can't now anyway, with your internship still going on."

"No, I can't leave until I've finished. Even if I

wanted to." They both knew he didn't want to, but he didn't think he needed to add that point.

"Yes, exactly. I know," she rushed to assure him. "The thing is, we've been having our differences lately." She shifted uneasily in her seat and toyed with a strand of her hair. "You're always so serious about everything. I mean, I admire you being a doctor and all that. But, well…you know me. I'm just not that way. I like to go out, meet new people, have fun. You know what I mean…." Her voice trailed off and she glanced at him again.

"I understand what you're trying to say, Lisa." He took a breath, about to say more, but she rushed on ahead of him.

"Well, good. I knew you would. I've just been thinking that maybe it's time for a break. For both of us. And this seems like the right time to face it, with me practically moving to California. Long-distance relationships never work out, we both know that. Besides, I really need to concentrate on my career now. This is my big break. I have to make the most of it." She paused a moment and turned her green eyes to him in a misty, imploring gaze. "It's hard for me to say these things to you, Jared. You've always been so sweet…. But please try to forgive me?"

"I do understand," he said again. "And there's nothing to forgive. Honestly."

He understood that—ironically enough—she was breaking up with him. She wanted her freedom. To be free to meet and date whomever she pleased out in

Hollywood, he guessed, though Lisa hadn't said as much. But he knew that was part of it, too. He felt an unexpected sting. *But it's just my ego,* he realized. The feeling passed quickly, replaced by a wave of relief and certainty.

For the past two days—even longer—he'd been tearing himself apart, worried over sparing her feelings. Now *she* was dumping *him.* Jared thought he might laugh out loud but somehow managed to restrain himself.

He leaned across the table and took her hand. "Lisa…it's okay," he said quietly. "I have to be honest with you. I've been thinking along the same lines myself the past few weeks. I don't think it's anyone's fault. But you and I…well, we're on different paths. We want different things out of life. It's taken me a while to see that, I guess. But now it seems very clear. I know how much this chance means to you. I know you're dreaming of a whole new life for yourself, and that's okay. I wish you luck. Truly."

Lisa stared back at him, looking surprised at his response. "Well…that was easier than I thought…I guess you have been thinking about this, too."

"And I think it's all for the best. For both of us."

She glanced at him again and he wondered if she now felt a bit insulted. She must have expected that he wouldn't let her go so easily.

The waiter arrived with their entrée, a timely interruption, Jared thought. He felt a sudden burst of appetite and was eager to dig into his *steak au poivre* and *pommes frites.* Lisa had ordered a grilled-salmon dish and now took a testing bite.

"They say salmon is good for your complexion. It gives you a glow."

Jared had not heard this latest health claim but didn't argue with her. "Well, you'll be glowing for your audition tomorrow. You'll glow them right off their seats."

Lisa smiled. "I hope so…." She paused and turned her attention back to her food, a thoughtful expression on her face. Suddenly she looked up at him again. "You're a good man, Jared. I could always rely on you. I'm going to miss that."

Jared didn't know what to say. She sounded wistful and he felt the same. But in his heart he knew they'd made the right decision tonight to go their separate ways.

"Well, we'll still be friends, I hope. Someday I'll be able to tell everyone I dated a famous movie star."

Lisa smiled broadly and Jared noticed the dreamy, ambitious gleam in her eyes again.

"Yes, someday you *definitely* will," she promised.

By the time Ket was through with her shift, she was tired and hungry. It had been a long day and she had resolutely turned her mind away from all thoughts of Jared Pierce and God's message to her. Now, as she moved toward the cafeteria, anxious to get something to eat, she felt a surge of pride. "Well, I was able to keep my mind on my work today. That's more than I've been able to do lately."

Moving along the line, she ordered the pork chops and smiled at Susie, the helper, saying, "Are these real turnip greens or just old ugly spinach?"

Susie grinned. "These are real turnip greens! You never had better," Susie promised. "And look, we have sweet potatoes today, too."

"I'd better have some."

After loading her tray down and pampering herself by accepting a wedge of coconut pie, Ket paid for the food, and looked for a place to sit. The cafeteria was crowded but she spotted an empty space over by the wall. Quickly she moved to take it before anyone could beat her. It was at a table for two and she did not know the woman who occupied the other seat.

"Is this seat taken?" Ket asked.

"No, sit right down." The woman looked up for a moment from the book she was reading then returned to it.

Ket sat down, asked a blessing over the food and began to eat.

The food was delicious, but she ate slowly. She was thinking of a difficult medical case that she had been dealing with, then her mind moved to Denny Ray Kelland. She had visited him as usual that day and spoken with Dr. Bjelland but there was no positive news.

She was vaguely aware that the woman at her table had finished her meal and had gotten up to leave, but Ket's mind was on Denny Ray and she paid little heed to the busy hum of the cafeteria.

Immersed in her thoughts, she started when a voice said, "Mind if I join you, Ket?"

Turning quickly, Ket saw Jared standing beside her, a tray in his hands.

"Of course not. I can use the company," she replied. She saw that he had only a bowl of soup and an apple on his tray. "That's not much lunch for a working man."

"Not really very hungry."

Ket attempted to keep up a conversation, but Jared's answers were monosyllables. She'd felt a bout of nerves when he'd appeared, and now the knots in her stomach increased so much she lost her appetite. Yet something told her not to take his reticence personally. She sensed he was distracted, perhaps even worried about something serious. She finally fell silent, whereupon Jared shrugged his shoulders and gave her a wry smile. "Not very good company, am I?"

"Something troubling you, Jared?" she asked quietly.

For a moment Jared hesitated, then said tentatively, "I guess so."

"Want to talk about it?"

"It's just a personal problem."

"I guess most of our problems are personal."

Jared suddenly laughed. "You know, I never heard anyone say, 'Hey, I've got an *impersonal* problem.'" He picked up a cracker and stared at it. "I've always pretty much handled my own problems."

"That's admirable, but maybe not always a good idea," Ket said. "I often go to my dad or mom with mine."

"You're lucky to have someone."

"Surely you have a friend?"

"Not really. I know lots of people, but you can't dump your problems on just anyone."

For a moment Ket hesitated wondering if she were saying the wrong thing. "What about Lisa? Can't you talk to her about it?"

Jared put his fork down. "No." The single monosyllable was not curt but somehow very final. "Lisa and I broke up."

"Oh…I'm sorry. That's too bad." She felt caught off balance and didn't know what else to say. His tone had been so flat and matter-of-fact. If he felt bad about it all, he certainly wasn't showing it, she thought.

Jared shrugged. "It was all for the best. We both thought so. Lisa has gone out to California, to be an actress in the movies. I think she might make a go of it, actually. We just didn't want the same things out of life. It's better to see that now rather than later, don't you think?"

"Oh…sure. Absolutely," Ketura agreed quickly. "I'm sorry, though," she said again. "I didn't mean to pry."

"That's okay. You didn't pry. It will be all over the hospital soon anyway—it's such a gossip mill around here."

Jared glanced over at Ket and realized he liked what he saw. There was an openness in her, a habitual repose, and he thought of how few women he knew who had that quality. She was, he knew, a girl with vitality and strength, and there was a fire in her that made her attractive in his eyes. *I've been thinking about her as a little girl—as she was when we played together,* he thought suddenly, *but she's a woman now, with all a woman's softness and mystery.* She smiled at him and he realized he felt better talking to her. An impulse took him. "If you're finished, maybe you'd like to go out and watch the fish?"

Ket looked surprised. "All right," she said. He rose first and politely pulled out her chair. "I always like to come out to the fountain and watch the fish," Jared remarked, as they walked out to the courtyard.

"I do, too," Ket answered.

They had reached the fountain and sat down on one of the cypress benches. The pool was smooth and unruffled, mirroring the pale blue sky and the fleecy white clouds that drifted overhead. A huge carp surfaced, his mouth gaping.

"Nothing for you, fish," Jared murmured. "See me later." He turned to Ket, smiled and let his hand fall naturally on her shoulder. "Ketura Lindsey—psychologist."

"All personal problems solved—we never close," Ket responded, acutely aware of the light pressure of his hand on her shoulder.

"I was a monster when we were growing up." Jared shook his head, a rueful expression in his eyes. "I was rotten to you."

"We had some pretty heated arguments, didn't we?"

"I always liked your name."

"You never told me that."

"Ketura—she was Abraham's second wife," he said.

"Not many people know that."

"I've always found that part of the Bible interesting, especially the story of Abraham. That fellow was quite a man. He married Ketura after Sarah died and he was ninetysomething years old. Then he had a lot of children by Ketura."

"That's right. He did."

"Odd thing. You don't see many ninety-year-olds starting families. God does some peculiar things, doesn't He?"

"Yes, He does."

Ket was breathing more easily. The sunbeams had turned the eastern skies into a pale shade of amethyst, even darker indigo near the skyline. The warm breezes caressed her cheek and the sound of the fountain was soothing. She said suddenly, "I enjoyed your testimony in church."

"Oh, were you there? I'm afraid I'm not much of a testimony giver. I was there just because of Lisa."

"I know, but really your testimony meant a lot to me." She hesitated, then said, "I saw you hit the home run that won the national championship."

Now Jared Pierce was astonished. "Did you really?"

"I thought you were the best player I ever saw. If you hadn't gotten hurt, I believe you'd be playing in the majors right now."

"I like to think that myself." Pierce grinned. "But it didn't work out that way."

"Does it bother you sometimes that you got hurt and couldn't play professional ball?"

"It did at first, but I don't think about it anymore. Did you ever want to be anything besides a nurse?"

Ketura shook her head. "Not really. I always wanted to help people. I'll be happy to get my R.N." She hesitated, then said, "You were there when the missionary from India spoke, weren't you?"

"Well, you have been keeping up with me."

"I was sitting right behind you."

"You went forward when he called for those who were bound for India, didn't you?"

"Yes."

"I remember now." He seemed intrigued by the idea and leaned closer to her. "You're going as soon as you finish your training?"

"It'll be up to the mission board, but I'm anxious to go."

"Tell me about it. I've never understood missionaries. It's such a hard life. You have to give up so much."

Ket haltingly began to speak. She told him how God had been working in her life since she was an adolescent. First leading her to nursing school and then finally revealing that He was going to use her as a missionary in India. Finally she looked up, surprised the sky had grown almost dark. "Oh, I've kept you too long!"

"Not a bit. Where are you headed? Are you through with your shift?"

"I am," said Ketura. "I was just going to go home."

"I'm finished, too. I wonder if you would mind giving me a ride home. My car is in the shop for the afternoon, and I'm getting off sooner than I expected."

"Of course I'll drive you home."

* * *

As she pulled into her driveway, the drive home was a blur for Ket, but she went over and over what had happened when she dropped him off.

She had parked and was waiting for him to get out of the car, when he suddenly took her hand and held it firmly. Startled, she had looked at him and saw that he was smiling at her. "What is it?"

"You are good medicine, Ketura. Just like Denny Ray said."

"Good medicine?"

"Yes." The pressure of his hand increased and suddenly he kissed her hand, then laughed at her look of shock. "Remember how all this started? I was looking for a friend to tell my troubles to."

"Why—that's right!" Ket's voice was filled with surprise. "We never did get around to talking about that, did we?"

"No, but it's all right. Somehow all my worries just flew away." He got out of the car, then before closing the door leaned over and gave her a smile. "I'll remember this—if I get another case of the blues, I'll know who to bring them to. Good night, Ketura."

"Good night, Jared."

Sitting in her driveway, a glimmer of hope came to her for the first time. "God, maybe You're right after all. It just couldn't have been an accident—that he would come to that one table and that was the only place for a seat," she whispered.

She sat there for another long moment. *I'm glad he likes my name*, she thought. She smiled then, a strange secret smile, got out and went into the house.

Chapter Nine

The sound of Ket's pen across the paper made a faint scratching sound. She liked to write in her journal with a real fountain pen. It was part of her daily life to use ballpoint pens, for that was common practice in the medical world. She had discovered, however, that there was something pleasurable about writing with a pen that had a nib and dispersed real ink. She had more than a dozen of them at home and used different ones, some that wrote with a broad line, others with a fine spiderweblike line.

Real fountain pens were more trouble than ballpoint. When a ballpoint ceased to write, you simply threw it away and picked another one from a stock. It was almost like picking an arrow from a sheaf of arrows. It was the throwaway society with a vengeance.

But Ket now found it satisfying to watch the smooth lines flow out of the pen as she wrote steadily across the page. True, fountain pens sometimes malfunctioned. They had to be cleaned, the ink was easy to smear. Still, somehow it pleased her and she studied the words that she had written.

June 27

I thought it was the beginning, but it was only an incident. We went out to the fountain and sat down, and he talked to me. It was almost sunset, and the last rays of the sun threw his features into relief. I don't think he knows how handsome he is—and that's a good thing! It isn't good for men to be pretty, but he's not that exactly. There's a strong manliness in him. He's very rugged and masculine. He's one of those men that won't change much as he gets older, I think.

But what am I talking about? I sound like a high school sophomore talking about a high school quarterback! In any case, being with him was so…easy! His car was in the shop so I drove him home, and he asked a great many questions about India and about me. He is one of those people who are really interested in others. Sometimes you can tell when people are not. They ask the right questions, but you can look in their eyes and know they are actually all thinking about something else. But Jared isn't like that at all.

I told him I'd seen him in church and he was surprised about that. We didn't talk about any great theology, but he said enough that I know that he's a Christian. He told me that he wished he were a better one, and I said that we all wished that. I kept expecting him to say something about Lisa, but he didn't even mention her. In a way I was a little bit disappointed. They seem so mismatched, but I couldn't pry into his personal life.

But I've been disappointed. I thought that after we met that he would call. But he didn't. We passed in the hall and he's nodded and smiled, but nothing more. I suppose that's professional, but I am disappointed about it. In any case, it's as if to him it never happened, and I suppose I'm making too much of it. I was so excited thinking this was God's will and now nothing has happened. So, I'm a little bit depressed.

But God knows all of these things. It always helps me to know that God knows the end of every story. He knows what's going to happen in my life and He's always known it, even before the world was made. So, I'm a little bit depressed tonight but not terribly so. As Robert Browning said, "God's in His heaven—All's right with the world."

Ket read the last words over again, then shrugged and put the journal away, cleaned the nib of the pen and then went downstairs to start her day. Her mother was in the kitchen, drinking coffee as she read the morning paper. Bedford ran out from under the kitchen table and met her with joy—as if he hadn't seen her in months.

Stooping down, she roughed his fur. "I've got to go to work, Mother. I may be a little late tonight. Sally O'Brien has the flu and I'm taking her patients."

"All right, dear. I'll save supper for you."

"Don't do that. I'll grab a bite at the cafeteria."

She made the trip to the hospital quickly, and since she was early went at once to see Denny Ray. She tried to be as cheerful as she could, but there was something in his expression and in his eyes that she didn't like. He himself tried to be cheerful, she could tell, but he felt terrible. When she left, she went at once to Dr. Bjelland, and said, "Can you tell me anything about Denny Ray?"

"Nothing new. It's on the razor's edge. You know how these things are."

Ket got no satisfaction out of that and found herself thinking more and more about the young boy.

It was late in the day when suddenly Ket's friend Sally appeared ready for work.

"I thought you were sick."

"Oh, I guess it was one of those twenty-four-hour bugs. I'm all right. You don't have to cover for me anymore."

Actually Ket was glad enough to follow this advice. She changed clothes and went to the cafeteria for a cup of coffee. As she entered, she saw Jared sitting with his back to her, bent over a book. An impulse to go to him came, but she fought it off. Getting her coffee, she moved toward a table on the other end of the room but suddenly he looked up and saw her.

"Ketura," he called out. "Come over and join me."

Ket went over at once and sat down across from him. "Are you finished for the day?"

"Yes, I was filling in for one of the other nurses, but she came unexpectedly so I've got the afternoon off."

"So have I. One of the few times. Look what I have."

Ket looked at the book that he turned over for her and exclaimed, "Why, this is a book about India!"

"I got interested after I talked to you. It's quite a book. I skimmed through it, and now I'm going back reading it more carefully. There's a chapter in here on Mother Theresa."

"A wonderful woman indeed!"

Shaking his head, Jared said, "I just don't see how she could do it. Bathing lepers and taking people off the streets and cleaning them up. It's beyond me, Ketura."

"I remember reading about her once. She had taken a skeleton of a man in and he was filthy. She was cleaning him up and a reporter from the States was there. He watched her, the story said, and he said, 'I wouldn't do that for a million dollars.'" Ket smiled slightly. "And Mother Theresa said, 'I wouldn't, either.'"

Jared nodded with appreciation. "That's a good story. Probably true. Most of those stories are awful, but after reading this I can believe anything." He leaned back and examined her carefully. "And you really want to go do a thing like that? I believe God would have to speak very loudly to me before I followed that path."

"Yes. God's told me to go."

"Nice to get a clear mandate from the Lord." He reached out, took the coffee cup and looked into it. Watching the swirling liquid, he seemed preoccupied and did not speak for a time. When he did, he looked up and shook his head with a slight negative sign. "I wish I were as sure of my life as you are of yours."

"I thought you were. You're a doctor. After your internship and residency I mean."

"Sure, but *where* will I be a doctor? At one point, Lisa thought I would follow her to Hollywood. Or should I go where there is real need? Or should I just stay put?"

"I guess that all depends on what you want out of life. But I've always thought of you as a man who could make decisions and stick with them."

"Oh, I can do that all right, but that leaves God out of it, doesn't it? That won't do."

The two sat there talking for a while. He seemed to be frustrated about something, and finally he looked up and grinned. "Well, I guess I'm having kind of a pity party."

"A pity party? You mean you're feeling sorry for yourself?"

"I guess that's it."

Ket wanted to say, *You have so much. You shouldn't give in to despair.* Instead she said only, "Well, I guess we all have dark times, days when we feel uncertain and unhappy."

Suddenly he said, "You know what I do sometimes when I get into a mood like this?"

"I have no idea."

"I go to the zoo!"

Ket suddenly found that amusing. "Why do you do that?"

"Oh, I don't know! I just like watching the animals. It cheers me up. Some of them are funny and some of them are rather melancholy." He hesitated, then cocked his head to one side. "Want to go with me?"

"You mean now?"

Jared grinned at her. "I remember Mickey Mantle asked Yogi Berra what time is it, and Yogi looked at his watch and then asked, 'You mean *now?*'"

Ketura laughed. "Yogi didn't really say all those things."

"Probably not, but how about going to the zoo with me? Come on," he coaxed when she didn't answer right away. "It will be fun. We both need a break from this place."

"All right. I'd like to."

He got up at once, and said, "Let's take my car. I'll bring you back here afterward."

The visit to the zoo was a strange experience for Ket. She had never really liked zoos; although she liked animals she hated to see them cooped up. She said as much when they were watching the lions, and Jared observed, "They probably have a lot easier life in here than they have in the wild. I read a book once that talked about how many diseases and how many injuries they get, and no care, of course.

Why, here if one of these fellows get a toothache, I understand a dentist comes and gives him first-class treatment."

"I suppose that's true," Ket murmured. They were watching two young, black-maned lions who were wrestling below. "They look like kittens, don't they?"

"Pretty big kittens, but yes, they do."

They stood side by side, leaning on the rail and, for some time, watched the lions. There was a relaxed silence between them, Ket realized. She didn't feel tense, or a need to talk all the time with Jared, like she did with some men.

"You know, I saw a program about lions on TV the other night. It seems like pretty much the female lions do all the work," Jared said finally.

"They haven't heard about women's liberation, I guess."

"Nope, apparently not. According to the TV program they do all the hunting, have all the cubs. All he does is be a papa and stroll around showing off that big mane of his and getting into a fight once in a while."

"Sounds like some families I know of."

Jared laughed. He seemed to be enjoying himself, his dark mood having passed. "Come on. Let's go look at the monkeys."

They moved over to the monkey exhibit, which was mostly outside.

Ket was fascinated by the gibbons. "Look how they swing! That must be marvelous to be able to swing through the tress like that."

"I suppose so. Look, that sign says Gorillas. Let's go take a look at those big fellows."

The gorillas were there—indeed a male and a female.

"Wow, that one must weight five hundred pounds! Look at the arms on him!"

Ket was fascinated, as well. There was a tire in the cage and the big gorilla glared at them and squashed the tire as if it were made out of foam rubber. "I wonder if they're vicious?"

"Not from what I hear about it. They're really shy and aren't aggressive unless somebody troubles them."

Ket thought that must be true. Their expressions seemed so deep and thoughtful—so humanlike.

They moved on around the zoo and soon sat down on a bench. Ket bought some cotton candy and soon it was all over her face. "I don't know why I eat this stuff. It's such a mess."

"I don't know why you eat it, either. There's nothing in it. You bite it and then it's gone. I guess there's some kind of philosophical lesson in that, maybe theological."

"What do you mean, Jared?"

"Why, I mean a lot of life's like that. Think how pretty those cotton candy things look. All fluffy and sweet but then you try to bite, or chew it, or do something with it, and it's nothing. No substance. I think some people are like that."

"You're being a little bit unkind, aren't you?"

He looked at her quickly. "I suppose I am. Maybe I'm talking about myself more than anybody else."

"Jared, I don't understand you. You've got everything and yet you're unhappy." She tossed the cotton candy into a barrel then turned back to him. "Life's been very good to you. Think of all your blessings."

"I know it. I've got my health, a good profession, all I need in the way of material things." He hesitated and for a moment Ket wondered what he was thinking. "I don't know what's wrong with me," he said finally. He sat silently for a while and then added, "Somehow I can't quit thinking about that book on India." He turned to her and put his arm around her, letting his hand fall on her shoulder. "You could do that, Ketura. Go to India and live under those impossible conditions. I'm not sure I could, even if God told me to."

Ket was very much aware of his hand, strong and warm on her shoulder. She did not move, but said only, "I believe you could, Jared." She hesitated then smiled. "I believe you could do anything you put your mind to."

Surprised by this endorsement, Jared squeezed her shoulder. "I'm glad you think so. You and my mother. That makes two." He hesitated, then said, "You've made this a very nice afternoon for me, Ketura."

"It's been nice for me, too."

He met her gaze. "I haven't bored you with my woes again…have I?"

She shook her head. "No, not at all…. I like talking to you."

"You're good to talk to…but I've told you that before." He smiled at her. "When you get to India, I don't suppose there'll be any zoos. They let the animals run loose in the streets, don't they?"

"The cows at least, but I hadn't even thought about that."

Jared pulled his hand away and then stood up. "I guess we'd better go," he said regretfully. He studied her for a moment, admiring her fair complexion. Her skin was smooth and clear, bare of makeup, with a dash of color high on her cheeks from the sun and a charming sprinkle of freckles across the bridge of her nose. Her long composed mouth curved in an attractive line.

Ket rose and followed him to the car. He took her back to the hospital and seemed strangely silent. When they arrived there, he got out and went with her until she got inside her own vehicle. She turned to say, "Thanks for the afternoon."

He put out his hand suddenly and she put her own in it. He was looking at her in a peculiar way, and said, "Well, we'll have to go visit the animals again sometime."

"That would be fun."

His hand was warm and large and very strong, and he did not let her go. Just when she thought he'd turn her hand loose, he suddenly reached out and turned it over and examined it. "Good strong hands," he murmured.

"That's one thing I am—strong. It's a good thing. My sisters got all the beauty and I got all the brute strength."

Jared looked at her and started to say something, then changed his mind. "Good night, Ketura. I'll see you tomorrow."

She watched as he drove away. "That was odd," she said. "I don't understand him. He has everything, yet he's not happy." She started the car and moved out of the parking lot, turning down the main road. Dallas was beginning to light up already, and as she made her way down the interstate, she wondered what was inside Jared Pierce.

She drove home quickly and went to bed early that night. As usual she prayed, and for the third time she received what she knew was a message from the Lord. *Trust in Me. Be patient.*

"I do trust you, Lord," Ketura said aloud. "And I'm *trying* to be patient."

"Tell your friends you will soon marry."

Chapter Ten

For the next two days, Ket prayed hard and almost constantly, wanting to make certain the message that had come to her was truly from the Lord. Finally, on Thursday morning she woke feeling refreshed and clearheaded. She had complete confidence that God had again spoken.

But announcing to her friends that she expected to be married soon was another matter altogether. It had been hard enough confiding in her own parents. She knew that her closest friends—fellow nursing students Maggie, Debbie and Sally—were not that devout. They would probably decide she'd gone crazy—well, was working too hard at the very least—if she told them the complete and amazing truth.

Still Ketura knew she had to carry through on this latest request. She had to exercise faith and patience, as she'd promised herself.

But I don't have to tell them whom *I'm marrying—
not yet at least.* The realization calmed her nerves a bit.

She'd decided to tell her friends all at once, rather
than go through it separately with each of them. When,
how and where had remained the question. They met
for lunch practically every day, but the hospital cafeteria was about as private as a network newsroom.
Everyone in the world would hear her secret in no
time. Some comfortable setting away from the hospital would be best, she thought. The four of them hadn't
gotten together for dinner lately so it didn't take much
persuading on her part to arrange a night out at their
favorite Mexican restaurant. Thursday night had promised to work out the best for everyone, and her friends
all appreciated Ket's efforts to bring them together for
a relaxing night away from the hospital.

Ket was the only one who dreaded the event. More
than once, she'd nearly concocted some excuse to
avoid joining them. Wednesday night she'd tossed and
turned. After doing so for over an hour, she'd sat bolt
upright in bed and said, "This is not what God wants!"

Turning on the bedside lamp, she'd picked up her
Bible and had held it unopened as she prayed aloud,
"Lord, I don't want to be one who has to have a miracle or a sign before I obey—but I need to be *absolutely*
certain that I'm doing the right thing. Please show me
something from Your Word that will drive away these
doubts!" Opening the bible she leafed through it
slowly, not reading it by chapters, but simply reading
verses she'd highlighted in the past. All of them had

meant something to her, and she'd memorized most of them.

For over an hour she read, praying for a verse to catch at her. Finally her eyes fell on the words "Be careful for nothing, but in everything by prayer and supplication with thanksgiving, let your requests be made known unto God. And the peace of God that passeth all understanding shall keep your hearts and minds through Christ Jesus."

Ket stopped dead, still noting the date she'd inked in beside the verse, and it all came back. "Why, this is the verse that came to me when I was so filled with doubt about India!" she whispered. And she remembered how disturbed she'd been—and how this verse had brought peace to her. It had been like water to someone dying of thirst! Now she read it aloud, and then broke it up into parts as was her habit.

"If I'll do three things—pray, supplicate and give thanks—God will give me peace." She read the verse again and again, taking each word, asking for wisdom to understand. Finally she said, "I've been praying and I've been supplicating—but I haven't been giving thanks. That's exactly what happened when I had such doubts about whether God was calling me to India!"

Closing the Bible, she'd held it and had prayed aloud, "Dear Lord, I ask pardon for doubting You—and for forgetting how You have helped me in the past when I had doubts. Right now I give You thanks—for giving me guidance and for dealing with me with such loving kindness. Thank You for promising me a husband. Thank You for giving me a man of God to share life with me. By faith I claim the Word You have put into my heart!"

Placing the Bible on the table, Ket had turned out the light and had drifted off into a deep sleep.

At precisely seven Thursday night, Ket found herself surrounded by her three closest friends and knew there was no escape. While her friends chatted and examined their menus, Ket sat quietly. She scanned the menu, but felt so nervous she could hardly read a word. Luckily, she'd been at this restaurant so often, she almost knew the menu by heart. The waitress came to take their order and Ket asked for her favorite, chicken fajitas, feeling she would hardly eat a bite.

Her friends loved to talk, as Ket well knew, and tonight was no exception. The conversation jumped from topic to topic—bossy doctors and cranky supervisors, shopping at the new outlet mall, studying for one more certification exam, dieting tips and Maggie's new haircut. No one seemed to notice that Ket was unusually quiet. Finally, as Ket expected, the talk turned to dating and eligible young men.

Debbie suddenly leaned forward, an excited gleam in her eyes. "Did you hear Jared Pierce dumped Miss Texas?"

"I heard that *she* did the dumping," Maggie challenged her.

"Who cares who dumped whom? Dr. Cutie is a free

man. That's all that matters to me. Maybe I'll skip this ice-cream sundae after all," Sally added, pushing her dish away. "Come on, ladies. There must be more."

"I don't know all the details, of course, but sounds like Miss Texas wanted to be free to seek her fame and fortune in Hollywood," Maggie said. "I hear she's auditioning for a part in a movie or something."

Sally laughed. "I wouldn't give up Jared Pierce if they offered me top billing."

"Me, either," Maggie agreed. "I almost feel sorry for the poor guy, though. He'll have every woman in the hospital chasing him now," she added. "Even worse than before, I mean."

"Well, I personally know of at least two—who will remain anonymous, of course." Debbie cast a teasing grin at Sally and Maggie. "How about you, Ket? Are you going to join the club?"

"Um…sorry…what club is this?" Ket swallowed hard. At the mere mention of Jared's name she'd gone into a panicked fit of distraction and had missed half the conversation. Now she sat nervously spooning her uneaten dessert as her three friends stared at her.

"I just wanted to know if you'd give up Jared Pierce for a shot at Hollywood. We're taking a poll," Debbie replied.

Ketura nervously licked her lips, but didn't reply. "Haven't you been tuned in lately?" Sally prodded her. "Late-breaking news—Dr. Jared Pierce is single again. Women throughout Texas rejoice!"

"And it sounds like we're all interested. We just

want to know if you're adding your name to the list," Maggie finished, making the other two women laugh.

Ketura forced a smile. She met Maggie's keen gaze then quickly looked away.

If ever there was a time to tell them about my marriage plans, this is it, she thought.

God, please give me the right Words to do Your will, she silently prayed.

"What's the matter, Ket? Are you feeling okay?" Debbie asked kindly. "You hardly touched your food…."

"Oh, she's all right," Sally insisted. "Just the thought of dating Dr. Pierce does that to a person. I'm feeling a little dizzy myself."

"Don't be silly. It wasn't that at all." Ketura smiled again, this time for real. She forced herself to continue, not knowing what she was going to say. "I'm sorry if I seem a little distracted tonight. It's just that…I have something to tell you guys. Something important."

Her friends stared at her curiously, and then at each other. "Something good?" Debbie asked quietly.

Ket nodded. "Yes…*definitely* good."

"*Definitely* good? Must be about a guy," Sally deduced. "You've met somebody, right?"

Ket drew in a deep breath. Well, this was going to be easier than she'd thought. Before she could add anything more, Maggie leaned over and squeezed her arm.

"Look at that grin. Aren't you the sly one? Why didn't you tell us, Ket?"

"Well…I am telling you. Right now." Ket smiled at them brightly. "I've met someone. I guess you could say it's…it's…*serious*."

Again her friends stared at her, this time in disbelief. Sally's mouth hung open for a moment and she closed it abruptly. "As in 'Here's a diamond ring' and 'Till death do us part' kind of serious?"

"Um…yup. That kind." Ketura sat up straight and stared straight ahead, trying hard to avoid their shocked expressions.

"I called you here because I want to ask you to be—" She faltered for a moment and then cleared her throat, and said firmly, "To be my bridesmaids."

If Ketura Lindsey had announced that she was going to the moon on the shuttle, her three friends could not have been more shocked. They reacted exactly the same. All stared at Ket for a moment, then all three began babbling at the same time, peppering her with questions. "Who is he? Where did you meet him? Why didn't you tell us about him?"

Ket sat there letting the questions roll off of her and she waited until Maggie said, "Well, come on! Don't sit there like a mummy! Give us the story!"

"It's really sort of a secret engagement," she said. "I—I can't even tell you who it is."

"Can't tell us who it is!" Maggie said with astonishment. "I can't believe this! You're about to get married and you won't even tell us who the guy is?"

"I'd like to—but I can't right now. Someday you'll understand why."

"You can tell us," Sally urged. "We won't tell anybody."

Ket glanced at her friends' eager expressions and was tempted to share the whole story. Keeping her secret grew harder every day and these women were her nearest and dearest pals. But finally she decided not to tell all right now. Maybe someday, but not tonight. Her friends might find the notion of talking to God more than fantastic and unbelievable. They might find it downright…odd. Ket knew they would never cause her problems at the hospital on purpose, but if the full story ever reached some of her nursing supervisors, she might have trouble completing her certification. She didn't need some hospital board deciding she was mentally unstable and unfit to continue her career.

"I'm sorry…but I can't," she finally replied.

She stumbled over her words, feeling she'd let them down. Sally looked insulted and Maggie sat back in her seat, seeming annoyed and hurt.

Only Debbie still wore a smile. She reached over and rubbed Ket's shoulder. "Sure, we understand. You must have some agreement with your guy, right? We don't want to force you to break a promise to *him*…do we?" she asked the others.

Sally grumbled some reply, but Ket could hardly tell what she said. Maggie just sighed, avoiding her gaze.

"I know it's frustrating for you. It is for me, too. Honestly," Ket said. "I'm sorry. But I did need to tell you."

Nobody spoke for a moment and Ket wondered if she'd done more harm than good by telling them she'd soon be married.

"Well…I guess it's okay, as long as you give us plenty of advanced warning about the wedding. I need a few weeks to shop for my dress." Maggie relented with a small smile.

"And lose a few pounds," Sally added, making them all laugh again.

"It's great news. I'm so happy for you, Ket." Debbie leaned over and gave her a hug. Then her other friends did the same.

"Can we tell people?" Sally's voice held a desperate edge. "You know me, Ket. I can do anything but keep a secret."

"I wish you wouldn't say anything for a while, if you don't mind. I hope it won't be for too long," Ket promised. "But could you please not tell anyone else for now?"

Her friends complained a bit, but in the end all three agreed to keep her secret. Ket spotted the waitress approaching with the check and picked it up before any of the others had a chance.

"Just for being such great friends, I'm treating all of you," she announced.

"Come on, Ket. You don't have to do that," Debbie protested.

"Let's share like we always do," Maggie chimed in.

"No, not this time. I really want to." Ket shook her head and took out her credit card.

"It's okay with me." Sally shrugged. "The bride can treat her future bridesmaids, you know. Don't forget, we'll be giving her a shower soon."

The others laughed. Ket only smiled. Choosing bridesmaids? A bridal shower? Whoa! The very idea gave her goose bumps. Would all of that really come to pass?

Faith and patience, she reminded herself. *Tonight I've taken another step forward. Who knows what tomorrow will bring?*

The next morning brought more surprises—some beyond Ketura's wildest hopes. She'd just begun her workday when Jared suddenly appeared by her side as she walked down the hallway pushing an IV rack. Lost in her thoughts, she hadn't heard him approach and nearly jumped out of her skin as he touched her arm to say hello.

"Jared…what are you doing up here?" Not the sweetest greeting, she realized.

Jared smiled, amused by her surprise. "Looking for you. Got time to have lunch with me?" he murmured.

"Why…yes. I suppose I could," she said carefully, trying hard not to look as shocked as she felt. "I mean, I'd really like that."

"Me, too. But let's skip the cafeteria if you don't mind. I'm pretty bored with the menu…and the other customers, come to think about it."

Ket laughed. "I know what you mean. Where would you like to go?"

"Oh…I don't know. I'm an intern, remember? I don't get out much." His warm smile charmed her. "Maybe you know a place. Something quiet, where we can just relax and talk. With good food, of course."

He looked hungry already, Ketura thought with amusement. "I know just the place. I'll meet you outside at twelve-fifteen. Is that good?"

"Perfect." He smiled at her again, then with a small wave, turned at the end of the hallway. Ketura smiled back, then turned in the opposite direction. She pushed the rack along, feeling as if she were suddenly walking on air.

At precisely twelve-fifteen, Ketura stepped outside the front entrance of the hospital and found Jared waiting there. "I have my car today," he said. "I'll drive."

"It's only a few blocks away. We can walk if you like."

"Great. I love to walk. In fact, I'll race you."

Jared was teasing her again, but she enjoyed it. He quickened his pace and she did, too—daring him to outwalk her. It almost amounted to a race, and Jared was somewhat shocked at the way she kept up with him. "I've never seen a woman that could keep up with me!"

"My legs are longer than yours."

Jared, being six foot five, laughed at her explanation. "No, they're not! But you're a great walker for a woman."

"I always outwalk most boys. I could outrun a lot of them, too. I was always big and rather awkward growing up."

"Well, you certainly outgrew that stage."

Surprised at his comment and admiring tone, Ket glanced at him. They had both changed out of their hospital greens, and he was wearing a white shirt and a pair of loose-fitting gray slacks. She wore a pair of tan slacks and peach-colored sweater set.

"This is it," she said when they reached a small restaurant amidst several businesses that lined both sides of the street.

"It looks like a telephone booth."

"It's bigger on the inside. See the name? Old England."

When they went inside, Ket was greeted at once by Esther Spencer, who spoke with a broad, British accent. "I'm pleased to see you, Ketura."

"This is my friend, Dr. Pierce. Dr. Pierce, this is Esther Spencer. She's the owner."

"Your usual table is free, Ketura. Come along."

It was, indeed, small inside, accommodating no more than eight tables. Along one side was a glass case behind which a tall, sandy-haired man grinned and nodded. "That's my husband, Tim. This is Dr. Pierce."

"Hi, Doc," Tim said. "I got this pain in my side whenever I lift my arm. What do you think I ought to do about it?"

Accustomed to this kind of teasing, Jared said, "Don't lift that arm. My bill will be in the mail."

Tim laughed. "Thanks a lot! You medical types are always helpful."

The tables were covered with white linen tablecloths, and the silver was real, and the tea that Esther brought without asking was served in genuine delft china.

"What will it be today?"

"I'll have whatever is good."

"I think I'll have the same." Jared grinned. "It's nice to see such trust in cooking. I wish my patients trusted me that much."

"Esther and Tim never fail."

They waited for their food, drinking the hot tea and taking turns talking mostly about inconsequential things.

Looking around, Jared announced, "I like this place. It's small."

"Yes, it is. Don't you like big restaurants?"

"I don't like big anythings—big cities, big cars, big ice-cream cones. I think little is better."

"You don't really mean that!"

"Sure I do! Back in the good old days before we were brainwashed by TV commercials, we had good sense enough to appreciate small things. Not today. Everything has to be supersize, or jumbo...or grande."

"So, you're opposed to large servings at fast-food restaurants—that sort of thing?" Ket knew just what he meant, but asked anyway, just to see his animated expression and his eyes sparkle brightly as he put forward his points.

"Exactly! *Big* food. *Big* stores. *Big* gas-guzzling SUVs—a waste of our natural resources. And why does anyone need to go to a movie theater and buy a soft drink cup that holds a half gallon of soda, and get a container of popcorn as big as a bathtub?"

"—while watching a movie that cost a zillion dollars to film?"

"That's *just* what I mean," Jared agreed heartily. "I knew you'd understand. Not everyone would, of course." He met her gaze and smiled into her eyes. Ket felt warm inside, a special connection.

"Maybe you should go into politics. Start a movement. I have a good slogan for you—think small."

Jared put his teacup down and laughed. "I like it…but I'm not sure it will catch on. I'll try being a doctor first, see how that works out."

Ket smiled. "Seems to me it's working out just fine so far. From what I hear, I mean." She didn't need to say more. They both knew that the nurses heard all the reviews about the interns from the supervising physicians and even from the patients.

"Thanks, Ket. That's nice of you to say." He paused, suddenly looking thoughtful. "I'm just starting to realize it could take a lifetime to learn how to be a good doctor. It's more than what you've memorized out of books. More than what you learn hands-on as an intern or even as a resident. Patients are more than just bodies in need of repair."

"Their spirits need healing, too," Ket offered.

They talked more until the meal came, which proved to be excellent—roast beef tenderloin, potato pie with an artichoke bottom, a fresh dandelion salad and chocolate ice cream.

They ate heartily, and finally it was Ket who said, "I think we'd better be getting back."

"I guess so." Regretfully Jared toyed with the spoon, then took the last bite of ice cream. "Won't you miss American cooking in India?"

"I don't think that's very important. A man who goes into the service misses his mother's cooking."

"I suppose so."

It seemed to Ket that there was some sort of cloud hanging over Jared. He had been full of enthusiasm, and she had been pleased at his humor. Now she leaned forward and said, "What's the matter? You seem depressed."

"Oh, it's the same old thing we talked about." He shook his head, tossed his spoon in the bowl and said, "I just wish I knew where I was going—like you do."

Ket did not know how to answer that. She considered his expression, then said, "I think God will tell you, but we have to be open for Him to speak."

"Has God ever really told you to do anything specific—I mean, besides going to India as a missionary?"

Ket swallowed hard and blinked. *What a question! And coming from him, of all people.*

She stared at Jared, almost blurting out Yes, he told me that I'm going to marry you! However, she immediately shelved that idea, saying merely, "Yes, once or twice I've been very sure about what God has said."

Jared stared gloomily. "You're lucky. Well, let's get back."

They did go back, but to her surprise during the following week he asked her out to lunch twice. They went to the same restaurant both times. By the third time it had become almost a tradition, and she glowed with the notion that things were working out.

On Thursday, as they walked back to the hospital, he said, "I think I've been unfair to you, Ketura."

"How do you mean unfair?"

"Well, it's fine to eat lunch together. That restaurant is charming and we certainly find a lot to talk about. But there's more to life than Old England, Ket. And you never let me pay. How about a real date tonight?"

Ket sat still as a candle in a crypt. These past few days, she felt she'd gotten to know Jared so much better. He was right; they did have so much to talk about. But so far, his interest had only seemed the friendly kind. Ket had developed friendships like this with men before, only to be disappointed later. She knew that men often found her the perfect "pal," but when it came to asking someone out for Saturday night, she wasn't even on the list. She'd promised herself she wouldn't fall into that trap again, misreading signals and getting her feelings hurt. She wouldn't fool herself that these lunches together proved anything. She'd waited and watched, longing for him to show just a glimmer of something more.

Well, this was it. He'd asked for a real date! That

was definitely something more…even more than she'd hoped for.

"I'd like to very much," she said finally. She felt a sense of quiet triumph. And gratitude. *Thank you, Lord,* she said silently.

Her patience had been rewarded.

Quizzically he glanced at her, saying, "I don't even know what you like. How about going to the opera?"

"I've never been. Have you?"

"No, but I always planned to someday."

"I'd rather do something else if it's all the same to you."

Relief washed across his face. He smiled, his white teeth very bright against the golden tan. "I was just showing off. I wanted you to think I was cultured. What would you really like to do?"

"Almost anything but the opera."

"How about a baseball game?"

"I'd love it!" Ket said quickly. "But I doubt if we can get tickets for tonight."

"Doesn't matter. I've got season tickets, two of them."

"I warn you, I get a little bit carried away. I've been known to knock a hot dog out of my neighbor's hand when somebody hits a home run or the catcher picks somebody off."

"Good! We'll go and stuff ourselves with hot dogs and scream our heads off!"

Chapter Eleven

Jared turned the wheel of his red hatchback, inching along carefully in the bumper-to-bumper traffic that led up to the stadium. "Wow, look at this crowd. The game must be sold out."

"I think everyone wants to watch Steve Reed pitch against Roy Hatfield. It's some matchup. Reed has that knuckle ball. It's practically unhittable. But Hatfield's stats are awesome. I think he has the lowest ERA in the league this season."

Jared glanced over at her; his eyebrows jumped up a notch. He'd rarely heard a woman talk so knowingly about baseball, and he'd definitely never dated one who did.

"But we have the heavy-hitters on our side," he reminded her. "Sylvester, Grady and Lopez. They're all batting close to .300 or higher. What do you think, Ket? Will good pitching beat good hitting?"

He watched as she carefully considered the question. Finally she grinned at him. "I don't know if I'd go that far...but it certainly helps."

Jared laughed. "You sound like Yogi Berra now," he teased.

"Yogi Berra made a lot of sense sometimes. In his way," she countered.

"How true." He smiled at her again and turned his attention back to his driving. He was having a good time already, and they hadn't even gotten inside the stadium yet.

The two continued to talk baseball while parking the car and walking the long distance through the crowded lot to the stadium entrance. Once again Jared noticed he didn't need to slow his steps for Ketura's benefit. Her long legs matched his pace easily. She looked good tonight, he thought, dressed in a long denim skirt, a pale pink V-neck T-shirt with a white sweater tossed over her shoulders. She had on low-heeled white sandals, he noticed. Pretty, but sensible footwear for a ballpark. Her eyes were brilliant and her hair was loose, blowing in the breeze. There was an excitement in her, Jared noticed, and could not help thinking of the time he'd managed to drag Lisa here. She had been bored out of her skull and insisted on leaving in the middle of a no-hitter. "Nothing's happening! The score's nothing to nothing!" she'd said. "I want to see home runs!" Jared could not explain that a pitcher's duel was the most exciting kind of baseball for the real connoisseur and had never offered to bring her back—nor had she ever asked him to.

Now, as they joined the crowd that streamed toward the stadium, he was happy. "I love this stadium," he said. It was a beautiful stadium, rising from the rolling hills that surrounded it. The gates were labeled Third Base, Home Plate and First Base. "You'll love our seats," he added. "They're right behind home plate. You can really see those pitches break."

They passed through the turnstile and were immediately surrounded by the noisy crowd that had come for the game. Baseball crowds, Ket always felt, were different from other crowds. She could not explain it, but the people seemed to be neighbors somehow or other.

Jared said, "Let's take the escalator. My old legs are worn-out."

"You're just a wimp! Come on, let's take the stairs," Ket insisted. She took his arm and pulled him along as he protested.

"I'm an old man. You young folks have to consider your elders."

She stared up at him thinking how strange it was to look up to a man. At five-eleven she either looked directly into the eyes of most men or down, but Jared was pleasantly above her level. It made her feel somehow feminine.

As they entered the corridor that led to the inner realm of the stadium, as always when she stepped out, it gave her a thrill.

"There's something about the symmetrical green of

the grass, the Astroturf, showing up in tiny squares, the pitcher's mound rising out of the ground and the brown dirt of it contrasting with the emerald-green." She took in the bases and thought again, *It was a stroke of genius to make those bases ninety feet apart. If they were ten feet closer, there'd be too many people getting on. If they were ten feet farther, nobody would ever get on.* It was just exactly right for a speedy runner to beat out an infield hit.

"Here we are. One twenty-six and one twenty-seven," Jared said.

"Wow—these are *great* seats," Ket exclaimed as she sat down. "I can't wait to tell my dad. He won't believe it."

She suddenly felt self-conscious, thinking she sounded silly blurting out her thoughts so openly. But when she glanced over at Jared, he looked pleased. "Glad you like the view. Now, let's see who's warming up out there."

"Who's your favorite player on the team?"

"Danny Valdez," Ketura said instantly. Valdez was the stocky, muscular catcher, only twenty-five years old, but the best in professional baseball. He was always a danger at the plate when he came to hit, and his rifle arm could throw a man out at second without coming out of a crouch.

"Danny is great, all right. I think I like Rick Otley. He's such a powerful player. I'd hate to be pitching to him. I'd be afraid he'd knock the ball up my nose."

The two had such a good time talking but finally the

game started. Jared noticed that Ketura watched with complete concentration and barely said a word now, unless to comment on some event on the field. At the end of the first inning the home team was behind three to nothing and their unhittable pitcher was taken out.

"Looks like a loser," Jared said regretfully. "They aren't going to win tonight. They're just not hitting."

"Just you wait! They will!" Ket nodded vigorously. "They'll have Hatfield figured out by the time they've gone around twice, then you'll see."

"Tell you what," he said. "If you're right, I'll pay for dinner at the most expensive restaurant in Dallas. But if not, you can pay for the dinner."

"You're on," Ket said. "I don't consider this gambling because I know they're going to win."

The game proceeded and at one point Jared said, "We've got to have hot dogs. Can't go to a ball game without hot dogs."

He came back with two hot dogs and two soft drinks. As he sat down, Ket laughed. "See, while you were gone Valdez knocked a home run with two on so the score's tied. You're stuck for that dinner, Jared."

The game got so intense that when the home team relief pitcher struck out three men in a row, retiring the side, Ket squeezed her hot dog into a gooey mess.

"That's a nice hot dog you got there. It looks like someone stepped on it."

Ket looked down at the mangled hot dog and saw the ketchup all over her hands.

"I get so excited, I can't think!" she said. "I can't

eat this." She wrapped it up in a wad of napkins and looked at her hands. "I've got to go wash off."

"You'd better not. We'll fall behind again if you're not here to watch."

The game went into extra innings so that it was ten-thirty by the time Ketura said, "I told you they'd win! Four to three!"

"All right—all right! Don't rub it in! You've got more faith than I have. And you're a truer fan, I'll grant you that." He laughed. "Come on, I've got a surprise for you."

They got up and she followed him down the bleacher steps. He went to the players' level and led her straight out into the field. The guard there greeted him. "Hi, Jared. Good game."

"Sure was, Tom. Okay if we go in?"

"Go right on."

Ket was a little shocked as they stepped out onto the brilliantly lit field where the ballplayers still milled around. "Which one do you want to meet?" he asked, his eyes twinkling.

"I want to meet Danny, please."

"So be it." Taking her arm, he moved over to where the stocky catcher was talking with a teammate.

"I've got a fan of yours here, Danny. This is Miss Lindsey. She thinks you're the greatest thing that's happened to baseball since…hot dogs."

Valdez turned around and there was a warm glow in his eyes. He took the hand she held out and nodded. "Glad to meet you," he said. "Did you enjoy the game?"

"I always enjoy watching the team play. Even when you lose."

"I don't like to lose," Danny said. He released her hand and winked at his teammate, shortstop Bucky Willis. "If you hadn't dropped that ball in the first inning, we wouldn't have had so much trouble catching up."

Bucky Willis was a freckle-faced man of middle height who could run like a greyhound and catch anything that flew in the air. "You don't want to fool with this fellow. You know catchers don't last long, but I'll be around a long time," he teased.

"I hope you win the pennant this year and then the Series!" Ket said.

"That's the spirit," Bucky agreed.

"I like this girl, Jared," Danny said. "You ought to bring her around more."

The ballplayers spoke to her a few minutes more then turned to go into the dugout.

"That was so much fun! Aren't they nice?"

"Sure are. Times like this makes me wish I was still playing, but not really."

Ket thought of his words as she and Jared pressed out with the throngs until finally they got to the car. She seated herself and he got in, and said, "I never try to leave at once. You just have to stay in line."

"That's right. I do the same thing."

"Do you mean it when you say you're glad you're not playing pro ball? Most men would love it."

"Well, they play every day, and you really have to

have it in your blood. And as much as I admire some of them, it's a hard life, and I'd like for my life to account for a little more than hitting a baseball."

"Some of them do a lot with their money and celebrity. Some give away millions of dollars every year."

"Sure, you can do that, and I admire the guys that do share what they have with others."

They sat there talking quietly, waiting for the traffic to thin out, and as soon as they pulled out, he said, "I'm hungry. Let's get something to eat."

"I'm hungry, too," Ket said.

When he pulled into a Waffle House, she stared at him. "You mean, this is the most expensive restaurant in Dallas?"

"It's close," he said with a straight face. "Come on, let's have a waffle."

They went inside the restaurant, which was filled primarily with truckers it seemed. They ordered waffles, black coffee and sausages, and when the food came, Ket ate ravenously. "I'm going to weight three hundred pounds if I keep on like this!"

Eyeing her figure carefully, Jared said, "No, I don't think so. You look like you're just about right. I bet you're one of those women who never have to watch what they eat."

"Well, that's more or less right. I feel so sorry for Sally. She tells me she might as well just take ice-cream sundaes and apply them directly to her hips."

Laughing softly, Jared said, "I'm fortunate that way, too. But I still love to work out. It gets the stress out."

They sat there talking and the time passed and finally Ket stared at her watch. "Look at the time! It's midnight! I've got to get home!"

"Might as well stay up and watch the sun come up." Jared grinned, but he got up, politely pulled out her chair and they left after paying the bill at the cash register.

When they reached Ketura's house, Jared pulled up in front and shut the engine. This was the moment that usually made her nervous on dates, but for some strange reason, Ketura felt totally at ease with Jared. Maybe because they'd had such a great time.

"Thanks for a great night, Jared. If you ever need anyone to explain baseball to you again, let me know," she teased him.

"*Right.* Thanks for the offer." He laughed at her, then suddenly reached out and took her hand. "You'd be the first one I'd call. Not only are you a fountain of sports trivia, I can't remember when I've had so much fun. You suppose we could do this every night? Watch a ball game and then go eat waffles?"

A nice invitation, Ketura thought. At least he'd pictured her as part of his future. She smiled softly at him in the dim light, intensely aware of the warm pressure of his hand.

"Hmm… That's such a lovely idea," she said with a sigh. "But there's more to life than baseball and waffles."

"Yes…I know." He sat for a long moment without saying more and Ketura didn't say anything, either. She liked just sitting with him, feeling the strong, warm grip of his hand around hers.

Suddenly he turned to her again. "Well, I did have a great time tonight. It's just so much more fun to do something you love with someone who loves it as much as you do…. Does that make any sense to you?"

"It makes perfect sense. I feel the same way, actually."

"I took Lisa to a ball game once," he confided suddenly. "I'll spare you the grisly details. Let's just say the outing was a total disaster. Guess I should have known then it wasn't going to work out." He shook his head. "You have to keep searching, I guess. One man has to find the one woman in his life that will make him happy and that he can make happy."

The idea was romantic and idealistic, Ketura thought. But it didn't seem to bode well. He certainly enjoyed her company, and they did seem to have so much in common. But could Jared ever see her as the *one* woman in the world meant to be by his side forever? She doubted that would ever happen. She stared straight ahead, feeling suddenly deflated.

Faith and patience. The words popped into her head, snapping her out of her cloud of negativity.

"You think that's the way it is, Jared? One man, one woman?" she asked him.

"I'd like to think so," he replied. "I heard an old myth once that when God made a creature, He tore it in two and called half of it man and half of it woman. Then He scattered them all throughout the world. The man half and the woman half would only fit each other perfectly. They might match up with somebody else, but like tearing a sheet down the middle in a ragged pattern, there's one man and one woman that's perfect for one another. If you get someone else—" he shrugged "—you're going for second best. At least that's how the myth goes."

"Do you believe it, Jared?"

"I'd like to. What about you? Tell me all about your love life."

Ketura laughed. "Actually it would be very boring. I never got into the dating game, mostly because I wasn't asked."

"Oh, come on, that can't be true!"

"It is, though. I was always taller than all the boys, and I was terribly self-conscious. My dad used to practically take a stick to me. I can still hear him. 'Will you straighten up! You look like Quasimodo!'"

"Well, you're perfectly in style now. All the models are six feet or more. It doesn't bother you, does it?"

Ket suddenly smiled. "Not when I'm with a man who's six-five." *Oh, no. I can't believe I said that to him,* she thought.

Smiling, he reached over and put his arm around her, then turned her to face him. "You know, I'm about to break a promise that I made to my mother many years ago."

Ket was very aware of the pressure of his arm, but she did not try to move back. "What promise?" she asked curiously.

"I promised Mother that I'd never kiss a girl on the first date." An impish light leaped into his eyes; that hidden humor that she had noted in him was in full sway. "But I'm going to break my promise. Right now. It's all your fault, Ketura. You shouldn't be so beautiful, and smell so nice, and be so desirable."

Ket allowed him to pull her close and she was pressed tightly against his chest. She lay soft in his arms, her warmth a part of him. Her nearness filled him with a sense of awe and wonder.

Their kiss was a new experience for him, unchartered territory. She was a fire burning against him, and a wind somehow moving inside of him. She had not resisted and he savored the softness of her lips, the faint scent of lilac in her hair and subtle perfume that lingered on.

Suddenly her lips pulled away, breaking the tension, and he released her at once. Ketura had been shaken by the caress and for a moment could not speak. Jared watched her. He knew she had a curtain of reserve that sometimes broke out into a teasing expression. He knew also, somehow, that she was a woman with a great degree of vitality and imagination, but that she held them under careful restraint. Most of all, he knew that she was courageous, could face a life of difficulty. Her courage and simplicity were so very rare. He had never met anyone like her, for there was an enormous certainty in her, a positive will. And now as she faced him, the light in her eyes held some kind of question, and he asked, "What is it?"

"Nothing, Jared." Still stirred by his embrace, she said, "I've got to go in now—" She did not finish her sentence, and he responded quickly.

"You don't like for men to take liberties, do you?"

"I think that part of life is what God reserves for marriage. I guess it's old-fashioned but I've always believed that, Jared." She leaned forward suddenly and put her hand on his cheek. It was a bold gesture for Ketura. She had never expressed her feelings in such a way, and now she said rather huskily, "Whatever happens, I'll never forget tonight." She got out of the car and left him sitting there.

As she made her way into the house, she heard the car drive off. She went into her bedroom, where she undressed and went to bed. She could not sleep for thinking of the evening. She went over every part of it, enjoying it and savoring it, and finally she began to pray. And she ended by whispering, "God, I know You're working this out. That which seemed impossible to me."

And as happened before several times, she got a quick impression. *Go buy a wedding dress.*

Ketura lay there and then finally smiled. "It's no more daring than anything else I've done. I'll do it tomorrow, Lord."

Chapter Twelve

In the midst of all the activities of Mercy Hospital, which included all the complicated methods of healing the sick, another world coexisted. Somehow there was a line drawn between the patients and their families who spent part of their lives there, and those who made Mercy Hospital a living entity. This line was as sharply drawn as the Great Wall of China, for those who served as doctors, interns and staff occupied the highest realm, with the director of the hospital serving as much in the nature of the captain of a ship. His word was law, and he was generally feared by most of the staff. Beneath the director were the physicians, those with the coveted initials M.D. after their names.

Even this group was subdivided, however, for there were the residents who would be much like the barons in the European hierarchy. They oversaw the interns who were the lowest order of the qualified doctors.

The nurses, without whom the hospital could not have run, were much like the landed gentry. They well knew that without their help the hospital could not function and some of them became quite dictatorial, not only to the nurses under them but to the doctors themselves. An excellent nurse could get away with a lot indeed!

Then there were the technicians who ran the machines. They were like high priests laying hands on the complicated electronic devices, and had their own level in the life of the hospital.

Someone had to keep the hospital clean, someone had to cook the food and serve it. The multitude of duties carried out by these people were necessary for the existence of Mercy Hospital. Many of them took great pride in their work.

As Ket was filling out the endless paperwork her job required, it occurred to her that the hospital was like a finely tuned engine. As long as all the parts were operating as they should, there was a smoothness and efficiency about the operation. But as it only took one spark plug to impair the efficiency of a car, only one bit of grit in the carburetor, only one malfunction in the multitudinous bits, pieces and parts that made an engine run, so Mercy Hospital never was completely tuned so that it ran at one-hundred-percent efficiency.

Ket put the pen down and rubbed her eyes. It had been a long day. Her astigmatism was bothering her so she was wearing the black-framed glasses that she had for close work. She looked over now at Maggie Stone who was engaged in a vociferous argument with an X-ray technician. When Maggie got angry, it was as though electricity flowed out of her, and now her eyes were sparkling and her rather strident voice could carry, it seemed, through the whole sixth floor.

The technician was a tall, hulking man who towered over her. His name was, prosaically enough, Tom Jones, and he had little fear of the dire reprisals that Maggie was threatening him with. He had sandy hair about the same color as hers and mild, blue eyes.

"Aw, come on, Maggie, don't be mad at me. I'm working as fast as I can. I can't help it if these machines break down."

Maggie shook her head and her sandy hair popped out from under her cap. She did not push it in but waved her finger in his face as though it were a pistol. "I've got to have those X rays and you've been sitting on that blasted machine for two days now! Tom, I've got to have it and that's all!"

"Well, I can't promise that," Jones said. He scratched his head thoughtfully and then smiled. "But I'll tell you what I can do. I can take you out tonight. How about dinner and a movie? You like the movies, right?"

Maggie at once dropped her hand and said in a mild voice, altogether out of contrast to her former tone, "I love the movies. Like to eat, too. What time will you want to pick me up?"

"Maybe about six. You like Chinese food?"

"I love it!" She smiled then and Tom nodded, saying, "See you tonight, Maggie."

As soon as Tom Jones was gone, Ket smiled saying, "Well, I guess you taught him a thing or two, didn't you?"

Maggie turned quickly. "What are you talking about?"

"One minute you were going to turn him in to the director for inefficiency and slovenly work, and the next thing you're making a date to go out with him."

"That's another thing entirely," Maggie insisted. Then she smiled. "I always thought he was attractive. And he's a nice fellow. Something might come of it."

"You really like him?"

"Sure I like him. I'll tell you more after our date. It could be interesting." She came over and sat down beside Ket. Her eyes narrowed. "What's new with you?"

"Well, I bought a wedding dress yesterday."

"You're kidding me!"

"No, I really did. My mother and I picked it out."

"What does she think about this guy you're marrying?"

"She doesn't know any more about him than you do."

"I can't believe it! You're too much!" Maggie leaned back and straightened her cap, shoving her hair into place. "Look, you can tell me. I'm one of your best friends. I wouldn't tell anybody else," she whispered.

"I'm sorry, Maggie. I just can't."

"All three of us are busting to know who he is."

"You haven't told anybody I'm engaged, have you?"

"No, but it's been a struggle. And you know how the

gossip goes around here. If that ever got out, you'd be given the third degree."

"I know. That's why I don't want you to say anything." Ket closed the folder and stood up, saying, "I'm going to look in on Denny Ray. Cover for me, will you?"

"Sure. How's that kid getting along?"

"Not too well, I don't think. Dr. Bjelland won't say much."

"Well, he's always Gloomy Gus. That Denny Ray's a sweet kid. I wouldn't mind having a few like him myself someday."

"Neither would I. I won't be gone too long."

"You're not sneaking off to meet Prince Charming, are you?" Maggie grinned. "I wouldn't put it past you."

Ket merely smiled at her, turned, and left the floor. She took the elevator to the fourth floor and went at once to Denny Ray's room. She was surprised to see Jared step around the corner. He brightened up at once, and said, "What are you doing here? I thought you were on duty until six."

"I just came to see Denny Ray."

"Mind if I come along?"

"Not at all. That would be good, Jared."

The two made their way along the corridor, and as they walked he said, "Your favorite baseball team has been on a road trip. They'll be back Monday. Would you like to go? It's a night game."

"I'd like it a lot."

They had reached the door, Ket opened it quietly.

She saw Denny Ray propped up in bed. He was watching television. "Hi," he said wanly as she stepped in.

"Hi, Denny Ray, I brought Dr. Pierce with me."

"Hello, Denny Ray." Jared went over and stood on one side of the boy's bed while Ket stationed herself on the other.

"How are you feeling today?" Ket asked. She did not really need his answer, for she knew he was not feeling well. His eyes were dull, and there was a hollowness in his cheeks that she had not noticed before.

"Not too good," Denny Ray murmured. He looked up at Jared and said, "Are you going to poke at me some more?"

"No, I'm not here for an exam, Denny Ray. I just came for a visit."

Jared and Ket sat down and Denny Ray said, "I've been watching Super Sam. I've seen the videos so many times I know them by heart."

"I've got something you might enjoy, Denny Ray," Jared said quickly. "I love videos about animals, especially the National Geographic Society series. Would you like to see some of them?"

"Sure. I like to watch things about animals. Have you got the one where the cheetah runs down the deer?"

"I believe I have." Jared smirked. "It's a favorite of mine."

"I can't stand it!" Ket shuddered. "That poor deer!"

"You don't say, 'Oh, the poor little cow,' when you eat a hamburger." Jared grinned, then turned to Denny Ray. "I'll bring you a whole boxful tomorrow."

"Thanks. I'd like that."

"Do you have a favorite sport, Denny Ray?"

"I used to play baseball before I got sick."

"Is that right? What position?"

"First base."

"I played ball myself when I was just a little older than you."

"Did you play in the big leagues?"

"No." Jared laughed. "I wasn't that good. I got hurt and had to become a doctor instead."

"That's too bad," Denny Ray said, studying the tall doctor with interest. "I bet you wish you could have gone on and played in the majors."

"Well, not really. I enjoyed ball, but now I like to do other things. But when you get well, how about you and I take in a baseball game?"

A long silence came then and Denny Ray looked over toward Ket. "I don't know," he said slowly, "if I'm going to get well."

"Denny Ray, don't talk like that!" Ket said quickly. She leaned over the bed and put her arm around his thin shoulders.

"I feel so bad. I'm not getting any better at all."

"You mustn't give up, Denny Ray. You remember the sick people that Jesus found and healed? The blind, and the sick and the lame—and even the dead."

"But that was a long time ago."

"He's still the same Jesus today. He's just as alive as He was then."

"Then why don't He heal me now?"

It was an old question, and Ket's eyes met those of Jared who was watching quietly. "We never know about things like that. Sometimes in our suffering God is doing something that He can't do any other way. Look at Joseph, for example. You remember how we read about him last week? His own brothers threw him into a pit and were going to kill him, and he went to prison, and all kinds of terrible things happened."

"I remember that. He sure had a hard time."

"Yes, but at the end of the story you remember he became the highest-ranking official in the land except for the pharaoh, and he kept his people from starving to death and he saved his family."

"That's right, but I don't see that God could do anything like that with me."

Ket was at a loss to help Denny Ray. She had said everything she could and she empathized with his pain. As she stood there struggling, suddenly Jared began to speak. "I know it's tough, Denny Ray," he said. "You know when you're in a dentist chair getting a tooth filled, you think it'll never end. But it does. You've got a good gal out here. Nurse Ketura Lindsey is praying for you, she tells me. I don t know anybody I'd rather have praying for me than her." He went on speaking softly in an encouraging manner, and Ket was pleased to see that it meant a lot to the sick boy.

"Will you pray for me, too, Dr. Pierce?"

"I do pray for you, Denny Ray. How about if we pray right now?"

"Okay."

Ket took one of Denny Ray's hands and Jared took the other. He began to pray in a soft voice, and Ket found her eyes growing moist for she could feel the compassion in him. It was a side of him she had only glimpsed once or twice, but now saw clearly. *He's one of those doctors who really loves people,* she thought. *Not all of them do.*

Finally Jared ended his prayer then stood up and smiled. "I'll bring the videos by for you tomorrow, Denny Ray."

"Okay. That'll be good."

Jared was silent as they walked down the hall. "This sort of thing gives you a helpless feeling, doesn't it?"

"Yes, but God's able."

"Yes, He is." He hesitated, then said, "You're off tomorrow, aren't you?"

"Yes, I am." She wondered how he knew. He must have asked someone if she was scheduled to work on Saturday.

"Suppose we take a ride somewhere? Maybe to the zoo, or out to a lake. Someplace out of the city where we can just relax."

"That sounds great, Jared. I'd love to, honestly. But I promised to chaperone one of the youth groups from church to Adventure Land. There'll be about eight or nine of them. I'm dreading it. I love them, but they go wild as soon as they get inside."

"Could you use some help?"

"Oh, you wouldn't want to do that."

"Sure I would. I'm just a kid at heart."

Ket tried to dissuade him, but he was adamant. "I haven't been to Adventure Land in years. It'll be good for me. I love the rides, especially the scary ones. Will you go on some of them with me?"

"Yes. I love them, too." As Ket studied Jared's face she was aware that he had changed—and that made her very happy.

Chapter Thirteen

The late-night hours passed slowly. Jared's day with Ketura and the church youth group at Adventure Land had been fun, but exhausting. Still, he couldn't sleep. He'd finally given up, pulled on his bathrobe and tried to study some medical texts, a "never-fail" cure for insomnia. But even that remedy hadn't helped. He was all stirred up—images and feelings from the day swirling around his tired brain.

He still considered himself quite young, but being with teenagers made him remember what real youthful energy was all about. The kids had all been fairly well behaved, but probably more than Ketura could have handled on her own. He was glad he'd offered to go along and help her. Ketura had certainly been grateful.

They'd had a great day and just as he'd promised, they rode the Dragon Coaster together. He'd loved sitting close to her in the car, watching her eyes grow wide and hearing her shriek with terrified delight. He'd loved the way she'd squeezed his hand as the car slowly climbed a steep hill, and then buried her head in his shoulder as they came flying down the other side. He'd never enjoyed an amusement park so much as he had today, with Ketura. When he stopped to think about it, everything seemed better by her side; even the simplest pleasures, like eating an ice-cream cone or driving down the highway into a rosy-hued sunset. Lately he wondered how he'd ever gotten along before he'd met her. He'd been stumbling along through life, with his eyes half-closed, like a sleepwalker. She made him feel so much more aware, more alive—more grateful.

They'd dropped off the kids at the church, where they were met by the teens' parents. Then Jared took Ketura out for a quick bite, just a hamburger. They were both feeling logy from the amusement park and too tired to handle anything more. Though it was still early enough to catch a movie, Ketura had looked so beat that Jared drove her straight home. She fell asleep on the short ride from the restaurant, and she looked so lovely and peaceful, he hardly had the heart to wake her. Finally, he leaned over and gently touched her hair, then gave her a tender kiss on the cheek. Her eyes flew open with surprise, but she looked back at him with pleasure and a tender light in her eyes as she reached up and touched his face with her hand.

"Is this a dream?" she asked quietly.

"No…not at all."

"Feels like one," she answered.

He smiled down at her. "I know what you mean. But here…I'll prove it to you." Then he kissed her again, a slow, sweet, almost innocent kiss that somehow shook him to his core.

Ket finally pulled away, staring up at him. He could see she'd felt it, too.

How he longed to pull her back into his arms and savor her warmth and softness! Somehow he resisted. She was different from so many of the other women he'd dated. She was sweet and modest. Guileless, which made her all the more appealing to him. She was clearly less experienced with men, too, and he knew he had to be careful with her. Careful about her feelings. He didn't want to ever disappoint her.

More than that, she was special. He'd never realized how special until just these past weeks. She was unique. A gem. And he was determined to treat her that way.

Finally, he'd walked her to the front door and chastely kissed her on the brow.

Getting her out of his mind tonight was not that easy, though. She was never far from his thoughts lately. He wasn't sure how it had happened, but he knew he'd never quite felt this way about a woman before. What to do about those feelings was another question all together.

Jared closed his textbook abruptly and got up from his desk. He poured some milk into a saucepan, heated it slowly, then poured it out into a mug. Standing at the window, he stared outside and was mesmerized by the array of stars that spangled the heavens. Stepping out, he leaned forward and picked out the familiar constellations—Orion, the Big Dipper, the Lion. It always made him feel somehow significant. Some had said the immensity of space frightened them and made them feel small, but Jared always answered, "If God made all of this, then He's a mighty God. Space is simply proof of his immense, creative powers."

He finally lay on the couch, which was far too short for him, but he did not want to go back to bed again. He turned on his side, bent his knees and put his arm under his head. He lay there uncomfortably for a time thinking of Ket. He knew that there was a love for her in him. It had been growing slowly and he thought back to when they were children. He had always teased her then, as boys will tease girls, but he had found her always to be honest. He thought back over the high school days and all the dating games he had played. Not once had he ever asked Ket out, but now he was filled with the strange wish that he had done so.

"All the girls I went with, and not one of them had her character," he said aloud. He got up, rubbed his neck, which was stiff and painful, and stood in the middle of the room. "I wasn't looking for character in those days. I was looking to date the best-looking girl or the most popular girl. Ket was never any of that except for valedictorian and I wasn't around then." Ruefully he admitted, "I wasn't impressed by brains in

those days, just by pretty faces, nice clothes and pop-
ularity."

The night finally passed with Jared sleeping for perhaps two hours. He got up and staggered to the bath-
room where he showered, shaved and dressed. Leaving
his apartment, he went at once to church. He took a seat
in the balcony and joined in the worship rather absent-
mindedly. From where he sat he could see Ket in her
accustomed spot down close to the front. Her hair was
shining and he fancied he could hear her clear, alto
voice rising with the music to the balcony but he could
not be sure.

Finally the service was over and Jared lurked outside. He saw Ket say goodbye to her parents then head
for her own car. Wanting to have a word with her alone,
he waited until she was inside and her parents were
gone. Quickly he stepped in front of the car and came
around to the window.

"I didn't see you in church. Where were you,
Jared?" Ket asked with surprise.

"I was up in the balcony."

"What were you doing up there? Did you get here
late?"

"I've got to talk to you, Ket."

"Why—sure. Get in."

Ket waited until Jared folded his long length into the
car, and then said, "Why don't we go to the park? It's
quiet enough there on a Sunday afternoon."

"That's fine."

The park was almost empty, just a few strollers

going by. Jared followed Ket to a bench beside a large pond inhabited by flamingos and ducks. She asked, "Do you want to sit down?"

"Sure." Jared sat down beside Ket and draped his arm over the back of the bench. He stretched his legs out and was silent for so long that Ket said, "What's wrong?"

Turning to Ket, Jared said, "You know, I didn't sleep last night. I was thinking about—well, about you, Ket."

"About me?"

"Yes. I've never felt toward any woman the way I do toward you."

Despite the messages she'd been receiving from the Lord, Ket was stunned by this. "I don't know…what to say."

"I'm not surprised," Jared said wryly. He let his hand drop on her shoulder and squeezed it. "I've been so mixed-up that it's pitiful. A grown man not knowing his own mind!"

"About what?"

"Everything, pretty much." Jared shrugged. Her shoulder was strong under his fingers and he turned his eyes on her, saying, "I've been thinking all night about how I set my sights on the wrong things."

"What kind of wrong things?"

"Oh, nothing really bad. I'm not talking about becoming a doctor. I know God wants me to do that. I've always felt it, I think. I fooled around with the idea of earning my living playing baseball, but even if I hadn't been injured, I don't think I would have stuck with it.

But I'm not talking about that now. I mean back in school. I got caught up in the dating game."

"I remember that. I think you started out to date all the girls alphabetically. I guess Lindsey was too far down the line."

"Oh, it wasn't quite that bad!" Jared protested, then he suddenly removed his arm and locked his fingers together. "Yes, it was that bad, or worse. I wanted to date the most popular girls."

Ket laughed. "That's not unusual. That's why they're called 'popular.'"

"I'm serious, Ket. I think all my life I've been mixed-up about success. That's what was wrong between me and Lisa. We just saw things differently. She wants success in the worldly way and I'm convinced that's worthless. I had just a taste of that and it doesn't last."

"No, it doesn't. What do you want? Are you sure that you're not still in love with Lisa?"

"I never was," Jared said slowly. "Thought I was, but looking back on it now, it was just like trying to date the most popular girl in school. She was a beauty queen going to be a movie star, but that's not enough." He said in an understated tone, "She's not for me, Ket." He took a deep breath then reached out and took her hand and held it. "You're for me," he said.

Ket sat absolutely still. His hand was warm and strong on hers and there was something in his eyes that she had always longed to see in a man's eyes. It was love and respect and faithfulness, and for one moment she was tempted to simply throw her arms around him.

The same feelings had been building slowly inside of her, day by day, as she'd gotten to know him. She admired and respected him. She saw his goodness and worth. She saw him struggling to do right, to be generous and kind. To be a good doctor, to contribute and make a difference in the world. On so many topics, they shared the same view, the same values. Not the least of it, they could talk for hours on end, about serious matters, but also make each other laugh. Ketura could admit it now, even if only to herself. She loved Jared and would be the happiest woman alive if she could make her life with him.

Still, something was holding her back. While she was thrilled to hear him say he cared for her, the moment scared her, too. She suddenly felt so confused, so unsure of herself. Perhaps she simply wanted this too much and had wanted it for such a long time. Now that it was coming to pass, she couldn't believe it was real. The thought was so…overwhelming. She couldn't trust it.

She looked up and saw Jared watching her, still waiting for her response. She reached out and took his hand. "It's just that I feel…so confused."

Surprise washed across his handsome face. "Why, Ketura, you're the most levelheaded person I know. Don't tell me you're as mixed-up as I am."

"I want to say what I feel for you…but I'm afraid to."

Jared stared at her a moment, then looked away. She wondered if she'd hurt his feelings. It took courage to open your heart to another person, as he had just done. She could tell that she hadn't given him the answer he'd wanted…or expected. He stared down at her hand, which looked small held in his.

"I'm sorry," he said finally. "I didn't mean to shock you. Or rush you. I know that you haven't dated much and this is all new to you. It's new to me, too. Honestly. This has all happened so fast. Maybe I should've waited to tell you how I feel. But I just couldn't somehow." He shook his head, then looked up at her, meeting her gaze with a tender smile. "I think there's something good between us, Ketura. Something… wonderful, really. I know how I feel, in my heart. That's not going to change," he promised. "But it looks like we're both a little confused right now. Maybe we just need some time to get to know each other better and get used to the idea."

Ketura nodded. His words helped her feel more settled inside, more hopeful, too. Jared slipped his arm around her and pulled her close. She sighed and rested her head on his shoulder.

"There is something good between us. Something truly special," she said quietly. "Let's wait and see what God will do."

Chapter Fourteen

"Well, here he comes. Dr. Gorgeous to the rescue," Debbie murmured to her friend Sally. The two nurses were striding the hallway and had simultaneously caught sight of Jared walking toward them.

As if on cue, they both smiled and waved to him. He smiled back. But to their surprise, he slowed his pace and stopped to talk to them.

Ordinarily, Jared wouldn't have stopped to chat, but he knew the two young women were good friends of Ketura's. Blocking their way, he held up his hands. "Stop right there. You shall go no farther unless you can answer the question."

"This sounds like something out of a fairy tale," Debbie replied with a laugh.

"Yeah, it does. But he doesn't look much like a mean, angry troll, does he?" Sally's tone was serious as she peered up at the tall, handsome doctor.

"You've never seen me before my coffee in the morning, Sally," Jared replied. "Now here's the question—do either of you know where I can find Ketura?"

"Ket? Sure, she's down in the cafeteria on her break," Debbie replied.

Sally's entire expression suddenly brightened, as if a lightbulb had switched on in her brain. "Hey…are you two seeing each other or something?" she asked boldly.

Jared grinned. "That would be telling. You know what this place is like. A rumor like that can get blown up bigger than the state of Montana in no time. Besides, I thought I was asking the questions around here."

"I get one back since we gave you the right answer," Sally countered. "I thought you were still getting over Miss Texas. It's not good to rush into a new relationship so soon after a breakup, you know."

"So I've heard." Jared smiled and shook his head. Sally was outrageously forward and impudent, but he couldn't help find her amusing. She had a certain brash charm he was sure many men found attractive. "What are you trying to do, start a column for the lovelorn?"

"You can be my first client. Here's some advice for you, too. You'd better be careful about Ketura. She's engaged, you know. Well…practically."

Debbie suddenly gasped and jammed her elbow into the other woman's side. "Sally! That's a secret. You promised you wouldn't tell!"

Sally's eyes widened and she covered her mouth with her hand. "Oh, my! I didn't mean to let that slip out. Just pretend you didn't hear me, okay?"

Jared stared intently at the two women, his expression suddenly dark. "Ketura never told me she was engaged."

"Well, I wish I hadn't said anything, and I really don't know much. All I know is she told me, Maggie and Debbie that she was seeing someone and it was very serious, and she expects to be married soon. She's even bought the dress."

"A wedding dress?" He sounded shocked. Debbie sighed and stared at the ground. Sally nodded meekly.

"Haven't you said enough?" Debbie tugged at her friend's arm. "Come on. Let's go before you do any more damage."

"I guess I'm just a blabbermouth. Never could keep a secret. Heh, don't listen to me. Maybe it was just a joke," Sally said as Debbie tried to lead her away.

Jared's mouth drew in a hard line and he nodded as he turned away. *If this is all a joke, then the laugh is on me,* he thought grimly.

He stalked toward the Exit sign at the end of the hall, ran down two flights of stairs, then marched straight to the cafeteria. Several co-workers he passed on the way tried to catch his eye to say hello, but Jared ignored all of them. He was so upset, he could hardly see straight. He could not explain why for he was not a man given to a quick temper. Somehow, though, he felt betrayed. *It's not as if she was just dating someone else— that's different. But practically engaged and keeping it a secret! I thought she was the most honest young*

*woman in the world, but there's something wrong with
this. Maybe Sally got it wrong, but I'll have to find out.*

Entering the cafeteria, he saw Ketura sitting at a
table alone, reading a magazine and drinking coffee.
He went over to her. "Mind if I sit down, Ketura?" he
said brusquely.

Looking up with surprise, Ketura smiled. "Have a
seat. Do you want some coffee?"

"No, not right now." Pulling the chair back, Jared
sat down and studied Ket's face. As usual, she had a
slight smile and her eyes were frank and open.

But when he did not speak, she saw the tightness
around his eyes and lips. "What's wrong, Jared? Did
something happen?"

"Yes, something happened. I just heard a rumor. I
don't think it could be true, but I'm going to have to ask
you."

"A rumor? They're all over this hospital. What is it?"

"Your friend Sally just told me you're practically engaged. She says you expect to be married very soon.
That you've even bought a wedding gown."

Ket felt as though a land mine had suddenly gone
off under her feet. All the time she had been in Jared's
company she had longed to share with him some of the
things that were happening to her. It had been a struggle to keep her own counsel, but now she saw that he
was angry clear to the bone. But she still couldn't tell
him the truth. She was sure he would think that her
story was a preposterous, desperate lie.

"Well," he said almost harshly, leaning forward as

she did not answer immediately. "It's a simple question, Ketura. Yes or no?"

Ketura straightened up and lifted her chin. She was ashamed and humiliated, but even now Jared saw a hint of her will and her pride in her bright eyes and in the set of her lips. Something moved across her expression then, changing it, and he knew that beneath the pleasant contours of her face that she was having some sort of a struggle.

"Yes. I did tell her that."

"Congratulations! I guess you forgot to send me one of the engagement notices."

"Jared, it's not like it sounds!"

For a moment he studied her, then shook his head. "I don't understand it. I've never met a woman like you—or that's what I thought. But this is deceitful, Ket. All the time we've spent together lately. Why didn't you say something? Why didn't you at least give me a hint? Did you enjoy leading me on? Was it a game for you?"

Ket drew in a quick breath. "No…not at all. I mean, I wasn't leading you on. You don't understand, Jared…."

"Oh, I understand. Better than you think. Now I know why you seemed so upset on Sunday, when I told you how I felt. No wonder you felt so confused," he added harshly.

Ket stared at him, unable to answer. She felt numb with shock, as if the entire world had crashed down around her in the blink of an eye. Jared looked so angry and hurt. All because of her. What did it matter if she tried to defend herself? He wouldn't listen to her, he wouldn't believe her, she thought. She was sure that after today he'd never want to speak to her again.

"It's not like it sounds" was all she could manage to say.

He shook his head sadly and turned away. He didn't speak for a long moment, seeming lost in his own thoughts, his own misery. Finally he said, "You've disappointed me, Ket. You'll never know how much."

Then he rose abruptly and brushed past her, walking quickly through the crowd and out the door again.

Ketura sagged in her seat and held her head in her hands. She felt the tears well up in her eyes but didn't want the entire world to see her crying. Ever since she and Jared had started to get to know each other, she'd felt sure that voice behind her had been right. Now she knew that everything was wrong. She'd made a dreadful mistake and they were both going to suffer the humiliating, heartbreaking consequences.

Ketura returned to work and went about her duties, but she couldn't help hearing the echo in her mind. *You've disappointed me, Ket.* Nor could she help seeing the hurt in Jared's eyes. She herself was like a soldier who had been wounded but keeps on fighting. Sooner or later it would catch up to her as it did to them, but her self-discipline kept her going.

The day did not improve. That afternoon when she took time to make her daily visit to Denny Ray's room, she found Dr. Bjelland coming out. "What is it, Doctor?" she asked quickly.

Lars Bjelland stopped and shook his head. He gnawed his lower lip, then said in a voice hard and clipped, "The new medication isn't working. He's at the highest possible dosage. His condition deteriorates daily. We've got to operate on him or he won't make it."

"What are his chances?"

"You want to talk about chances, go to a horse race! Don't ask me, Ketura! I don't know. I've prayed and I know you have, and all I can say is it's in God's hands."

After Dr. Bjelland turned and walked off abruptly, Ket went in and kept Denny Ray company until his mother arrived. The boy was so listless, he didn't even want to play checkers or watch a video. Ketura read him a story and held his hand atop the covers. She said nothing of what Bjelland had said but did her best to cheer Denny Ray up. It was obvious to her, as it was to his mother who had fear in her eyes, that he was worse. Nevertheless, before she left, she said a prayer for him, then kissed him on the cheek and whispered, "Don't lose your hold on Jesus, Denny Ray. He's able."

Ket was driving home slowly, trying to keep her mind focused on the traffic. It was worse than usual, for evidently there was construction or a wreck down the way. The cars moved forward at a snail's pace while her nerves were screaming to get away, as far as she could from Mercy Hospital. Actually she did not even want to go home and the impulse came to her to take a sudden vacation. She knew, however, that that was impossible so she sat in the car as horns blew and drivers cut in and out of lanes, risking life and limb, but getting no closer to their destination.

She had been sitting there for over thirty minutes having gone no more than two miles when she suddenly realized that this would not do, and she began to pray.

Many times she had difficulty praying, but never like this. It was as if the heavens were brass and she could not get through it all. It was almost as if there were no God, and she was all alone in her own universe with no one to call upon.

Finally she began to quote Scripture, promises that she had used in the past, and slowly she felt a peace coming into her. She continued to pray, thanking God for taking away the anger and the fear and the humiliation that had come to her during her scene with Jared. She remembered a Scripture suddenly that said, "Only by pride cometh contention." She had never quite understood that verse but now she saw it.

My pride hurt, she realized. That's why I'm ready to strike out. When there's a fight, someone's always suffering with hurt pride.

She meditated on this for a while, slowly moving, until finally she was clear of the expressway. As she turned off and headed for home, she began to thank God for comforting her.

Then it happened! Just as it had before when she had

received the Word from God concerning getting married, it came creeping into her mind. At first it was just a stray thought and she brushed it aside immediately, saying, "That's just me."

But it came back again and again and kept getting stronger and stronger. It was a very simple thought. It consisted of one sentence. *Ask the pastor if he will perform the ceremony.*

Pulling into the driveway and struggling with this idea, Ket turned the engine off. She sat there for a moment, laid her head back against the rest and said in desperation, "Lord, Jared hates me! The pastor will want to know who it is, and if I tell him, I'll make things worse. Please don't make me do this!"

The answer, after a time, came, still gentle. *I will not make you do anything, but it would please Me if you would take another step of obedience.*

Wearily, Ket got out of the car and started for the house. She felt as if she were wading through a gumbo of mud, for every step was an effort. She was physically exhausted and emotionally drained. Still she knew there was nothing else to do, and she was as certain as she was the sun was in the sky that the next day she would be in the pastor's office asking him if he would perform a ceremony to a man who didn't know she had been promised by God to marry him—and who now totally despised her!

Chapter Fifteen

Now that the time had nearly come, Ket found herself thinking of the difficulties of the operation almost constantly. Finally she went to her father. With one quick glance he knew something was wrong. Without preamble Ket began to explain the situation that had developed with Jared Pierce. Laying his book aside, he listened as the words tumbled out of her, sometimes falteringly, sometimes as if she could not say them fast enough.

The house was quiet and Roger Lindsey remembered some long talks he had had with this youngest girl of his over the years. They had always been close—perhaps because Ket looked so much like him. Not that he didn't love his other daughters deeply for he did—but Ketura was his in a very special way that sometimes happened. Now he heaved a sigh and looked up at her. She was wearing a thin, blue cotton robe over her pajamas and her eyes were troubled. Always when she was upset or tense, a tiny crease appeared on her forehead, between her eyebrows. It was a flag that he learned to recognize long ago, and now he said gently, "It sounds like a bad day, Ket. But things always seem worse when we're right in the middle of them. You know that."

"Yes, but I'm right in the middle of it, and it's all tied up with my walk with the Lord."

Instantly Roger knew what she meant. "You mean because you're not certain at all now that these impressions you've been getting are from God?"

Gratefully Ket looked at her father, glad that there was one she could speak to this frankly. "That's right, Dad. If I've gone this far wrong about hearing God, how can I be sure about anything else?"

"You're not having doubts about your call to India, are you?"

For a brief moment Ket sat there. It was unlike her. One thing she had been certain of for years was that God was calling her to India. That she had to hesitate was a sign of how disturbed she was. "No, not really," she said. She lifted a hand and ran it through her hair adding thoughtfully, "I may have made a fool out of myself over this, but the surest thing in my life is that God wants me to serve Him there."

"Well, if that's the case, let's look at this situation." Roger leaned forward and said in a slow, even voice, "Either this thing is God, Ket, or it isn't. God doesn't give halfway commands. I can guess one reason why you're so troubled about all this."

"Why's that, Dad?"

"I think you may have been very attracted to Jared Pierce, in the natural, that is."

"Why, Dad—"

"Now hear me out. He's a fine-looking man and just your type. A baseball player and fan, a fine doctor, intelligent and, from what you tell me, has a good sense of humor. It's only natural that you would be attracted to him. Now isn't that so?"

"I guess you're right, but I didn't even think about marrying him until I got this Word from the Lord—so I thought—to marry him."

"But after that impression came, is it possible that it wasn't from God, but you were so attracted to him that you kept building on it? I just throw this out as a suggestion, Ket. I want us to get to the bottom of your problem."

For a long time Ket sat there thinking hard about the past. It was a way she had of turning the world off—going into her mind and analyzing situations. She was a strange combination, part romantic and part realist. As a realist she knew that she had had no chance at all of attracting a man like Jared, but as a romantic she had to admit that she was drawn to him. Finally she shook her head, saying, "I don't think so, Dad. As a matter of fact, I've fought about this impression about as hard as I've ever fought anything. I've told the Lord a hundred times that it's impossible."

"Yes, you did, but then that was early in your relationship. From what you said, after he started paying attention to you, even taking you out, that may have become a factor."

"I just thought it was God working it out." Ket spread her hands out helplessly in a vulnerable gesture. "I don't know, Dad. I just don't know what to do!"

The two sat there speaking quietly for half an hour. Ket knew there was nothing her father could do really, except to pray, and she finally said with a wan smile, "Well, I've got to go to work tomorrow and so do you. I wish you could wave a magic wand and fix me up." She got to her feet and he rose also. He stepped forward, put his arms around her and she murmured, "I'm a big trouble to you, Dad."

"No, you're not! You're the joy of my life, Ket." He kissed her on the cheek and noticed that she looked small and vulnerable, almost as she had when she had been a small child and had come to him with her problems. "I'm glad you came to me with this, Ket. Now we can pray together about it, and we will. Good night."

"Good night, Dad."

Ketura moved about her duties at the hospital as always, but she was aware that word of a "secret engagement" had gotten out. From most of the other nurses and interns she got merely wondering looks, but a few made teasing, even snide remarks.

The most difficult part was encountering Jared.

They had little occasion to speak, and when they met she was unable to even meet his eyes. She felt sure that he despised her. His words still burned into her mind, *You've disappointed me, Ket. You'll never know how much.* She could not get away from them, and felt miserable.

For the next few days, Ketura spent all her free time with Denny Ray. She would have done the same under any circumstances, but she knew that by visiting with her favorite patient she was also avoiding the gossiping tongues and curious stares down in the hospital cafeteria. One lunch break however, while Denny Ray was having tests to prepare for his surgery, Debbie and Maggie pressured Ket into joining them for lunch. Ket was reluctant, but she realized she couldn't hide away forever and had to face the rest of the world sooner or later.

She picked her lunch quickly, then met her friends at a table in a far corner. As she sat down, she spotted Jared on the other side of the room, sitting with Dr. Bjelland. He had lifted his eyes when she had entered the cafeteria and she met his gaze for a brief moment. He had neither smiled nor frowned but just studied her, then turned back to his conversation with Dr. Bjelland.

"Don't let it get you down, honey," Maggie whispered. "It seems bad now, but you'll get over it."

"That's easy for you to say," Debbie said. She was disturbed about Ket, for she had seen that her friend's spirit was quenched. Now she put her hand out and covered Ket's, saying with a smile, "I tell you what. Let's all get together and go out and do something wild and crazy, like ice skating!"

Ket knew her friend meant well, but didn't know what to say. She felt so hopeless, as if her heart was torn in two. She didn't see how ice skating could help. Before she could reply, Kirk Delgado walked up to their table. He stood over the three nurses and grinned. "Well, you haven't asked me to sing at your wedding, Ket."

The room went silent and Ket was sure that everyone was turning to face the little scene that was unfolding. Everyone she knew was waiting for her reply, and she felt her face flush with embarrassment. She felt like jumping up and running away, but knew that reaction would only look worse.

"Kirk, you're such a creep," Maggie said. "Why don't you find a deserted house and haunt it?"

Maggie's sharp rebuke only made his smile grow wider, Ket noticed. He was obviously enjoying making her miserable and basking in the attention of his audience. She let out a long breath, avoided looking at him and stared down at her half-eaten sandwich, willing him to disappear, but sensing he wasn't quite done.

"Cute, Maggie. Is that where you met your phantom fiancé, Ketura? In a haunted house?" he continued.

Ketura's eyes flew up and she stared at Kirk's nasty, gloating expression. She knew anything she might say in her own defense would only encourage him. She wondered if Jared was watching the scene from across the room, but couldn't bring herself to look over at him.

"Leave us alone, Kirk. Don't you have anything better to do?" Debbie said angrily. "Nobody wants to listen to you."

"Of course they do," Kirk jeered. "Everybody wants to know the truth about Ketura's secret engagement. Who's the lucky guy, Ket? I bet you don't even have a fiancé. You're just a lonely spinster who has to make one up...."

Ket was still staring down at the table, shriveled into her seat, while Debbie patted her shoulder and murmured comforting but indiscernible words. Kirk started to say something more when his taunts were abruptly cut off.

She looked up to see that Jared had grabbed Kirk's collar and suddenly whirled him around.

"That's enough, Kirk. Come along." The two men came face-to-face, Jared's mouth an angry white line.

"Hey! Let go of me!"

Jared didn't bother to answer. He gripped Kirk's forearm and led him from the cafeteria. Kirk struggled to get himself loose, but Jared had the advantage of height, weight and—clearly—determination. "Keep walking," Jared instructed him. "We need to talk. Privately."

The two interns disappeared through the swinging doors and Ket could feel all eyes upon her as a hush fell over the entire room. Then suddenly everybody started talking again. Talking about her, Ket figured.

"Thank goodness somebody got rid of him," Debbie whispered to Ket.

"Dr. Gorgeous versus Dr. Obnoxious. No contest," Maggie said.

Ket had no reply. It seemed more than amazing to her to see Jared come to her rescue. But Kirk's taunts were also embarrassing to him in a way, since it had gone around the hospital that they'd been seeing each other. It wasn't as if he was trying to protect her or anything, she reasoned.

Out in the hallway, Kirk continued to squirm, to no avail. Jared finally planted him against a wall a short distance from the cafeteria entrance. Kirk tried to walk away, but Jared rested a firm hand on his shoulder.

"Not so fast, pal. I haven't said what I have to say." His eyes flashed with anger and Kirk felt his mouth grow dry.

"All right," he stammered with false bravado. "Say it then."

"If you ever say one more word about Ketura, or ever dare speak to her again, about anything, you will be the sorriest man in Texas. I promise you." Jared's soft tone belied the rage Kirk could see plainly written on his face. "Do you understand me?"

Kirk shrugged. "Hey, I didn't mean anything by it. I was just—"

Kirk felt Jared's grip on his shoulder tighten. "Do you understand me?" he asked fiercely.

Kirk nodded. "Yeah, sure. I get it."

"End of discussion."

Kirk was suddenly released and slipped down, slack against the wall. He watched as Jared turned curtly on his heel and stalked down the hall. He felt an impulse to call out to him, to make an angry challenge. Then thought the better of it.

"I don't know what I ever saw in her," he mumbled to himself as he rubbed his shoulder and righted his clothing. "Some people around here are just plain...crazy."

For the rest of the day the hospital was abuzz with the rumors about the "fight." Ket was aware of them as she tried to work but did not do her duties well at all. She did not see Jared again that day, for which she was grateful. She could not understand his interference, for the sudden streak of anger that had leaped out of the man had surprised her. It was a side of him that she had never seen.

Somehow Ket made it through the day and left the hospital with relief. She did stop to check in on Denny Ray and found his parents maintaining a vigil beside his bed.

"Dr. Bjelland says he's come to a crisis," Bill Kelland said. He had not shaved and his face was drawn with fatigue. He glanced over at his wife who had fallen asleep sitting up in a chair. "He says that everything's been done. Denny Ray's got to have an operation." Ket shared Bill Kelland's anxiety and concern for Denny Ray, but tried hard not to show it. It wouldn't do Denny Ray's father any good if she sounded worried, too, she realized.

"Denny Ray's had excellent care, Mr. Kelland. The

very best. Everyone loves him so. We're all working as hard as we know how. But an operation is the only option left now. And I know Dr. Bjelland is trying to get Dr. Del Matson to fly in and do the surgery. He's the best pediatric cardiac surgeon in the world."

"I just don't see how we're going to make it if we lose him."

"You won't lose him. God won't let us down."

"You really believe that?"

"Yes, I do." Suddenly a thought came to Ket. "Look, you two have been here all last night and all day today. Go home and get some sleep."

"We can't leave Denny Ray alone!"

"I'll stay with him tonight. You get some sleep and come back in the morning. If Denny Ray's going to be operated on, you'll need your strength."

"Well—I guess I'd better take Ellen home. She's in bad shape."

Ket watched as Bill Kelland roused his wife and they made their way to leave. She said, "Don't forget. Nothing is impossible with God."

As soon as the pair had left, she took up station beside Denny Ray. He was asleep, but it was a fitful, erratic sleep, and he looked pathetically ill.

The hours dragged on slowly. Ket sat quietly for the most part beside Denny Ray studying his face and thinking how strange it was that such concern had come into her heart for one she had not seen until a few weeks ago. One of the older doctors had warned her, "Don't get too emotionally involved with your patients, especially the children. You know doctors and nurses have to keep their distance."

Ket knew this was the prevailing wisdom, but it didn't feel right to her, deep inside where it mattered most. "How can you keep from feeling for patients?" she wondered aloud. She knew some doctors and nurses apparently could arrive at this, but she herself was certain that she never would. She hadn't become a nurse just to remain detached and uninvolved.

The time moved slowly. Ketura got up at midnight and, seeing Denny Ray was asleep, went to get coffee. She returned and read the Bible, the one she'd given Denny Ray. Midnight came and then one o'clock, then two o'clock. She grew sleepy and as she was simply asking God to heal Denny Ray, she felt herself nodding off. She tried to resist, but she'd slept little the previous night and fatigue and lack of sleep caught up with her.

A sound awakened her and she stared, not knowing how long she had been asleep. She turned expecting to see another nurse coming in to check on Denny Ray, but then a shock ran through her as she saw it was Jared who had entered and come to stand beside her. She could not move for a moment, so startled she was and groggy from sleep.

"How is he?" Jared asked quietly.

"He's in the crisis period."

"I talked to Dr. Bjelland. He said not to give up hope."

Denny Ray opened his eyes suddenly. He was heavily sedated, but he smiled wanly, saying, "Hi, Doc, did you come to play ball?"

Jared reached over and took Denny Ray's hand. "Someday soon you and I are going to be playing ball together. I'm going to make you into the best first baseman in Little League."

Denny Ray looked over and saw Ket. He said, "Hi."

"Hi, Denny Ray."

He said no more but closed his eyes and went back to sleep.

They stood looking at each other for a moment, and then Jared moved around the bed and stood to face her. "Do you still believe that God's going to heal Denny Ray?"

"I guess there are always doubts, Jared, but yes. I do believe it."

"Somehow I do, too."

Again a silence fell on the room. Jared appeared awkward, Ket thought. She could not speak but could only wait.

"Ketura, I'm feeling rotten about the way I've treated you."

"No, you're not as bad as I feel, Jared. I humiliated you."

"Come sit down." They moved over to the windows and he pulled the extra chair closer to hers. When they'd seated themselves, he said, "I didn't give you a chance to explain anything. I just unloaded on you. I guess I was surprised. Shocked actually," he admitted. He looked down and stared directly into her eyes and she felt a deep, indescribable tug of affection for him. "Is there some explanation, Ketura?"

His tone was quiet and even, yet Ketura still heard a faint, poignant note of hope. She felt again a wave of sadness for having hurt him. *I've got to tell him the truth,* she thought. *Even if he thinks I'm insane.*

"Yes…there is an explanation. I want to tell you, Jared…."

"Ketura…are you still here?" A familiar voice made them both look up. Jared leaned back in his seat and Ketura stood up to see Paula Bellamy, the nurse on duty, enter the room.

"I'm still here…. Dr. Pierce just stopped in, too. To look at Denny Ray."

Paula glanced at Jared and then at Ketura. Ket could see that her colleague sensed there had been more going on than Jared checking on the patient, but she wasn't the gossiping or judgmental type. She cast Ket a mild smile and went about her duties, first taking Denny Ray's temperature so gently with a digital thermometer, the boy hardly stirred.

Jared's beeper suddenly sounded. Ketura saw Denny Ray stir and open his eyes. Paula smiled and greeted him as she slipped the blood pressure band around his arm.

"I've got to run." Jared checked the beeper and dropped it in his pocket again. "Are you staying here much longer?"

Ket nodded. "I promised the Kellands I'd stay all night. Until they return in the morning."

Jared's expression was unreadable in the dim light. "Well, maybe I'll catch you later then."

Before she could say anything in reply, he turned and left the room.

"Jared—" Ket called out, but he was gone.

She turned back to face Denny Ray who was watching her carefully. "Guess you like him a lot, huh?"

"Y-yes, I do, Denny Ray."

The boy reached out and took her hand. "Don't worry," he said, nodding confidently. "He's smart, you know." His face lit up and he added, "Hey, let's pray for me to get well—and for Dr. Pierce to fall in love with you. Then him and you can get married and live happily ever after."

Ketura Lindsey mustered a smile, though she didn't feel like laughing. "All right, Denny Ray. Let's pray for that."

The Kellands returned to the hospital at six o'clock and Ketura drove home watching the sunrise. She slept poorly, and went to work the next afternoon still tired. When she got to the hospital, she encountered Dr. Bjelland making his rounds. He said, "I'm disappointed in Dr. Pierce."

"Why—what makes you say that, Doctor?"

"He called me at the crack of dawn. Woke me before the alarm to say he had to take a couple of days off." Disapproval etched lines on Bjelland's face. "I thought I'd found a man I could depend on—but looks like I was wrong."

Ket wanted to defend Jared, but what could she say?

Deep down she knew that somehow she was partly responsible for Jared's behavior, but Dr. Bjelland would not listen to any excuses. A miserable feeling swept through her and she thought *I've made such a mess of things! I should have told him about what God has been doing in my life! Why didn't I?*

She wrestled with the answer to that all day, and finally she came to realize something. *I was afraid to tell him, because he might not believe it. He might laugh at me—and I couldn't bear that!*

Time passed on leaden feet, so it seemed to Ketura. She spent much time with Denny Ray and his parents knowing that they were all fearful. It was difficult for her to keep a cheery manner, but she managed as best as she could. "You're doing a good job with that kid, Nurse Lindsey," Dr. Bjelland said the night before the surgery. He suddenly put his hand on her shoulder. "I've warned doctors—and nurses—about getting too involved with patients—but I've learned something from this case."

"What's that, Doctor?"

"That a little love from a nurse—or a doctor—does more good than all the facts in the world!" He studied her, then asked abruptly, "What's with Jared?"

"I—I don't understand you."

"No? I think you do, Ket. You'd make a rotten poker player."

"A rotten poker player?"

"Yeah. You've got to be able to hide what's in your hand, keep your emotions inside instead of letting them show on your face." Bjelland studied Ket's face, admiring the fine bone structure. She wasn't pretty in the usual way, but in some other way she was quite beautiful. "I'm a pretty perceptive guy, Ket, and I've seen the way you look at Dr. Pierce."

Ket took a quick breath but when she tried to deny Lars Bjelland's words, she could not. "I—didn't know I was so easy to read," she whispered.

"He's a lucky guy," Dr. Bjelland murmured. "I was worried about that plastic beauty he was running with. But you two are right for each other."

"Do you really believe that, Dr. Bjelland?"

"Sure—and I'm never wrong about things like this!" A quick thought came to the doctor. "I'd guess that Jared's running away from something that's come up between you two—am I right?"

"Yes, I'm afraid so."

"Well, get with the program, Ket! Get it straightened out." Bjelland blinked, then said quickly, "Dr. Matson is due in on an early-morning flight. I had to do some wheeling and dealing to get him to operate on Denny Ray." He saw the expression in Ket's eyes, and said quietly, "He's the best there is for this kind of thing, Ket. Now—we'll just have to let him do his job, and believe that God will let us keep that young man around for a lot of years."

"Amen!"

"And—if you want me to speak to Jared…?"

"No!" Ket said quickly, and managed a small smile. "I'll speak to him as soon as I can."

Ketura was determined. She wouldn't wait until Jared returned to the hospital. She'd speak to him before that, she decided.

It was time to have a serious talk with Jared Pierce.

Chapter Sixteen

Once Ket had seen a movie about a doctor who contracted a serious disease. He had become a patient, and most of the movie showed how he slowly became aware of the callous treatment patients receive from doctors in hospitals. In the film the physician becomes angry and strikes out at the system. Ket had often thought of the movie, which had remained largely unheralded, but for the first time she was beginning to understand what the director and the actors were trying to do.

Ket had been around sick people in hospitals since her training began, but none of them had been family. She had a natural love and compassion, but somehow the plight of young Denny Ray Kelland had struck her harder than anything else since she had begun training. It was as if he were her own son, and she had thrown herself into intercession with a vigor that she had never known before. She prayed almost day and night and found herself, even when doing menial chores, praying a short prayer. *God, let Denny Ray get well.*

She met Denny Ray's parents in the waiting room at seven, right after Denny Ray was taken to be prepped. They both looked nervous and scared. They sat close together, holding hands, and Ket could tell that they'd both been crying.

The surgery was scheduled to begin at eight and would take at least four hours. The time passed slowly and Ket tried her best to give them some comfort. She concealed the anxiety that she herself suffered, though only with great effort.

At ten o'clock Dr. Bjelland appeared. Ket's heart leaped into her throat and she stood up with the Kellands. Seeing their fear, Bjelland smiled. "Just came to give you a brief progress report. Things are going well. Dr. Matson says he's never had things go as easily. Now, I've got to get back—but keep on praying."

Turning to Denny Ray's parents, Ket said with warm confidence. "It's going to be all right."

"Is that...usual?" Denny Ray's father asked. "For a doctor to give a report to the family in the middle of a surgery?"

"No, it's very unusual—but then, Dr. Bjelland's a very unusual doctor."

The three waited, watching the hands on the clock crawl slowly around, and finally at 12:32 p.m. Dr. Bjelland and Dr. Matson emerged. Ket took one look at the smiles on their faces and cried, "Glory to God! He's all right!"

"Indeed he is!" Dr. Matson beamed. He was a tall, lean man with gray hair and warm brown eyes. "Came through it like a trouper!"

"Thank God!" Denny Ray's parents exclaimed in one voice. Their faces were beaming and Ket stepped aside to let Dr. Matson give them the details. Her own heart was full, and Dr. Bjelland came to take her arm. "You can rest easy now," he murmured. "He's going to be fine. And I must say that both Dr. Matson and I believe that God's hand was in it. Everyone in the room gave a cheer when it was over. Almost like a revival meeting!"

"When can we see him?"

"Oh, in a few hours." Giving Ket a strange look, he asked, "Talk to Jared yet?"

Ket gave Dr. Bjelland a sudden smile. "No, but he's going to have a visit as soon as I can locate him. And he's going to hear some things that will surprise him!"

Ket changed into her uniform and reported to work on time. She worked her shift, checking on Denny Ray's progress during her breaks. Always the report was good, and she went into intensive care once to look down at him and murmur, "You're going to be fine, Denny Ray!" The sight of his regular breathing and the color in his face encouraged her greatly, and when she left the hospital, she was exhausted but at the same time a feeling of joy rushed through her.

Lord, You saved Denny Ray—now I need another miracle. Help me to make Jared understand what's been going on in my life!

Getting into her car she felt a sudden impulse—then set it aside. But as she left the parking lot she continued to feel that she should go by Jared's apartment. *It's too late—and I don't even know if he's there.* But still the impulse came. Finally she pulled over and picked up her cell phone. She dialed the number, expecting to get voice mail, but Jared's voice came to her strongly after the phone rang only twice.

"Hello?"

"Jared?"

"Yes—is this you, Ketura?"

"Yes. Jared—I know it's horribly late. Did I wake you?"

"No. Where are you?"

"I just got off from my shift, and—I felt I ought to call you."

Ket fully expected a rebuff, but Jared said at once, "I'd like to talk to you—if you're not too tired."

"Oh, not at all. Maybe we could go get a late snack. I could pick you up."

"I'll be outside waiting."

Ket was startled by Jared's willingness, and when she pulled up beside his apartment and he got into the car, she said, "I've got good news, Jared. Denny Ray is fine!"

"I know." Jared turned to face her, adding, "I called Dr. Bjelland this afternoon."

"Isn't it wonderful?"

"You know, I think that's exactly what it is, Ketura." Jared's voice was warm and he slapped his hands together in a sudden gesture. "We use that word *wonderful* so much we forget what it means—'full of wonder.' And that's what I feel about Denny Ray's surgery. It's full of wonder. God has to be in it!"

"I feel the same way." The two talked about Denny Ray, and finally Ket parked the car. Turning to face him, she said, "Jared, I've got something I have to tell you. I—I'm not sure how you'll take it, but I should have told you before this."

Ketura knew that she would have to tell everything. She began at the beginning and it went well until she got to one point. She had explained how God had told her how she was going to have a husband, and then later to tell her parents and then tell her friends she'd soon be married.

When she broke off and turned her face away, Jared reached out, put his hand on her cheek and pulled her back to where he could look into her eyes. "You're leaving something out, aren't you?"

"Yes. I don't know how to say this, but God told me—that you and I were going to be married, Jared."

There was a throbbing, it seemed, in Ket's ears, and she could not fathom the look on his face. His eyes were open wide and she watched intently to try to understand what he was thinking. He did not speak for so long, she whispered, "I'm sorry I let you in for all this, Jared."

Jared studied Ketura carefully. Something like a smile touched his broad lips. Then he said, "Do you still believe what God said?"

"God is always right," Ketura said simply. "Sometimes I make mistakes. Maybe I have about this, but I've done what I thought He told me to do, and the rest is up to Him."

Jared felt a sudden exultation. He reached out, pulled her toward him, put his arms around her and kissed her. His lips were warm and his arms held her strongly yet gently. He pulled his head back and looked down at her, saying, "I'll say one thing, Ketura Lindsey. No man would be bored being married to you!"

Ketura felt as if her heart was about to burst with joy. Her fears and doubts scattered like leaves in the wind. She'd opened her heart to Jared; she'd confessed her unbelievable story—and he believed her. And amazingly enough, forgiven her. She closed her eyes, savoring his embrace. She had a thought and whispered, "What about…India?"

"One miracle at a time, Ketura," Jared said quietly. "If God wants me to be your husband, I'm sure He can handle all the details."

Chapter Seventeen

On the second day after Denny Ray's surgery, Dr. Bjelland stepped into Denny Ray's room. Ket quickly stood up to face him, as did Bill and Ellen Kelland. Somehow they knew that this was a special visit.

Denny Ray was lying down, but his eyes were alert and he watched the doctor cautiously.

Dr. Bjelland suddenly smiled. "Good news." He waved the folder in his hand. "My, it's wonderful to be able to bring good news."

Ket suddenly felt very weak, as if she had to sit down again. "Thank you, Lord" was all that she could say, but she saw Bill turn to Ellen, hold her in his arms, murmuring something unintelligible. Dr. Bjelland walked over to Denny Ray and winked down at him. "See this folder? It means you've won! It's like the World Series! You're going to be fine, Denny Ray!"

The next few moments were rather confusing to all

of them. Dr. Bjelland explained how the operation had proved completely successful and the Kellands thanked him profusely. After he left Bill and Ellen turned to Ket. "I don't know what we would have done without you, Nurse Lindsey. You're a wonder!"

Ket's eyes were filled with tears and she dashed them away. "It was nothing," she whispered. She moved over to Denny Ray, reached out and hugged him. He was still weak, but his arms went around her neck, and he whispered, "God came through, didn't He?"

"Yes, He did."

"I knew it all the time," Denny Ray said, clinging to her. "Jesus told me."

"How did He tell you, Denny Ray?"

"I don't know how it was. He just told me, that's all."

"I guess it was kind of a voice behind you."

"Yeah, that's right! That's what it was. Kind of a voice behind me."

Word of Denny Ray's good prognosis went through the pediatric cardiac ward and then spread to other parts of the hospital.

Ket was as happy as she could ever remember. At the monthly staff luncheon, she felt a personal victory as Dr. Bjelland reviewed the history of the boy's illness. "We lose some, but when we win one like this one, I know that our work means something."

He glanced at Ketura and honored her with a special smile.

He would have said more, she thought, but at that

moment the door opened and Jared walked into the room. His eyes were bright and he walked straight to Ketura and stood by her chair. "Why, I didn't expect you back today, Dr. Pierce."

"You can't get rid of me that easy." Jared smiled. "I heard the good news about Denny Ray."

"Yes, absolutely wonderful prognosis," Dr. Bjelland said. "Won't you sit down, Dr. Pierce."

"No," Jared said. "I don't think I will."

A puzzled look swept across Dr. Bjelland's face. He glanced suddenly at Ketura who felt her face flushed with embarrassment. "Well," Dr. Bjelland said in a puzzled tone, "what do you want to do then?"

A few at the table reacted with laughter, but when Ketura quickly glanced at Jared she could see his expression remained solemn and focused.

"I've got a few remarks to make and something to do, and I want to do it publicly. That is if it's all right with you, Doctor," Jared replied.

Not knowing what else to say, the senior physician shrugged. "You have the floor, Dr. Pierce."

Ket was staring at Jared. He had given her one look and then turned to face Dr. Bjelland. Now he set himself squarely and there was a look of peace in his eyes. "I've had a couple of days off, as all of you know. We doctors have a pretty hard job. One crisis after another. I've been with most of you for a year, some of you two, some longer, and what I have to say, I want you all to know from me, directly. There have been enough rumors going around here."

Ket's heart suddenly seemed to grow tight. She could feel her own pulse beating. *What in the world was Jared up to?*

"I've been a Christian for a long time," Jared said, as if measuring each word. "But I've never really given the Lord first place. Well, something has come into my life recently that showed me that I'm missing something. So I took time out to go seek God, and that's where I've been for the past two days."

Suddenly Jared looked down at Ket again. He reached out and took her by the arm.

Ket felt herself grow pale, but he would not release her. She was pulled to her feet, and he took her by her hands and then suddenly smiled at her. "It's hard sometimes to know exactly what God has for us to do, but I know now my direction. Ket, God has told me that we are to be married. I love you very much, and I would be honored if you would be my wife."

Ket was not aware of the reaction that went around the table. Kirk Delgado had straightened up as if someone had struck him a blow. Maggie began to applaud and was soon joined by Debbie, then Sally joined in, then all the doctors suddenly were standing on their feet applauding. She was aware that they were calling out, "Hooray! Three cheers for Jared!" But she could only stare at him in wonder.

Jared leaned forward and kissed her gently, then said, "We've got a few details to work out." He looked around, and said, "I trust that you'll all excuse us."

Dr. Bjelland did not laugh often, being a rather serious man, but suddenly he began to giggle. "Oh, that's fine!" he said. 'Never mind that we've got a hospital to run here with a thousand patients. Just go on and carry on your little romance."

Ket felt herself being moved along by the force of Jared's grip. She left the room, and as soon as the door closed behind him, Dr. Bjelland turned to the three nurses and said, "I bet you three know something about all this. Women always know about things like this before men do."

"You bet your life we did," Sally said. She turned to her friends and smiled. "Looks like we'll be throwing Ket that bridal shower after all."

Outside in the empty corridor, Ket said nothing as Jared walked along beside her, his hand firmly holding her own. She was too emotional to speak. They left the hospital and walked quietly along until they came to the fountain. She turned to him, and said, "I don't know what to say, Jared."

"Say you'll marry me." He put his arms around her, kissed her and then said, "I love you as I never thought I'd love a woman."

And then something came to Ketura Lindsey. She knew that this was the man for her, the only one she could ever love. But she whispered, "But, Jared, what about India? I can't give up that."

"That's what I talked to God about."

"You prayed about going to India?"

"No, I prayed about doing anything that God wanted me to do, that's what I finally agreed to do. We've got more time here, and don't you think, Ketura, that if God wants me to go to India now that I'm listening to Him, He can shove me in that direction?"

Joy filled Ketura and she nodded. "Yes, He can," she whispered. She reached up, pulled his head down, kissed him. Happiness filled her, and she reached up and put her hand on his cheek. Staring into his eyes, she whispered with excitement, "It's going to be interesting being married to you, Jared Pierce!"

Epilogue

Ketura sat at her dressing table and brushed out her hair. Late-afternoon sunlight filtered through the sheer curtains. She'd been gone now nearly two years, but her parents had kept her bedroom almost unchanged, replacing the single bed with a sleep sofa so that the room was more comfortable for guests.

"But still a little Museum of Ketura," Jared had teased her when they'd first arrived back for their visit. She vaguely recalled flinging a pillow or maybe a slipper at him, but he'd merely ducked and laughed. She knew he wouldn't retaliate. Not in her condition.

She set the hairbrush down and stared at the gold band on her finger. It was often still hard for her to believe she was married to Jared. Sometimes she secretly felt like pinching herself. She'd found her old diary in a dresser drawer the other day and leafed through the pages, but she really didn't need to read those entries to remember. She often thought back to the way it had all unfolded and still felt as if she might be living in a dream.

Even after they had married and gone to India to work side by side as medical missionaries, the feeling continued. The work was the hardest she could ever imagine—taxing to her mind, body and spirit. She and Jared both faced sights and situations nearly every day that their training at Mercy Hospital had never prepared them for. But however grueling her duties, this had been her goal, to go where her skills were truly needed. To work hard and make a difference in the world.

Jared felt the same. They rarely needed to speak about it. That was only one part of what was so wonderful about being married to him. Once they'd opened their hearts to each other, it seemed that their lives fell into perfect harmony. It wasn't long after they'd gotten engaged that Jared decided he, too, had been called to be a missionary. Ketura knew that his realization had been a sincere one. Not just to please her, or because he felt he should follow her. She could see it in his eyes and hear it in his voice. He'd been led by the Lord to this work and felt grateful every day to have finally found a deeper purpose and meaning to his life.

So, even in India, working hard and living in hardship, they were deeply happy with their lives and with each other. In Ket's heart, she truly knew the peace of the Lord. The peace that surpasses understanding. While she loved coming back home and visiting with her family, she was often restless to return to their medical station once again.

But first, one small matter needed to be settled. Well, not that small a matter, she laughed to herself, as she touched her round, heavy belly. By the time they returned, they'd be a family. Ketura could hardly wait to hold her baby in her arms. Another reason she felt so restless, she guessed.

She heard Jared's step in the hallway and turned to see him enter the room. He smiled at her quizzically. "What are you doing up here, honey? Everyone's ready to go."

"Oh…is it time already?" Ket glanced at her watch, then back at her husband. "I didn't realize."

"We still need to pick up Denny Ray, and the stadium will be mobbed tonight. Reed is pitching, remember?"

Ket smiled. "I know. Just like our first date. He struck out nine that night, as I recall."

"I thought it was only eight…but you're probably right." Jared stood beside her and rubbed her shoulder. "Sure you're feeling up to it?" he asked tenderly.

"Absolutely! I wouldn't miss this game for anything," she insisted. She jumped to her feet, just to prove it.

Jared put his arms around her. "Not so fast…. I spent a small fortune on those tickets. At least you could give me a thank-you kiss."

Ketura tilted her face to his and circled her arms about his waist. "I guess it's worth at least one kiss," she teased him. "Are they good seats?"

He shook his head and kissed her deeply, and Ketura felt so loved and cherished, she had no more teasing remarks on her lips. She buried her head in his shoulder to hide her reaction.

"Sure you feel okay?" he murmured. "We could let you stay home and watch it on TV, you know."

"I feel all right.... I was just thinking, that's all."

"What about?" he asked quietly.

She didn't answer at first. Then she said, "About when you and I first got to know each other at the hospital... And when I heard God say I would marry you. I couldn't believe it. Sometimes I thought I was going crazy."

Jared pulled her closer and stroked her back with his hand. "I'm sure you did," he whispered. "But I thank the Lord every day that you had such strong faith, Ketura. I'm thankful every day that you believed and trusted Him."

Ketura didn't answer. She relaxed in her husband's warm embrace, concentrating on the sound of his steadily beating heart.

Suddenly, a major twinge in her belly made her jump. She looked up at Jared's shocked expression and laughed. "Just a little kick.... Don't worry. I'm not going to have our baby at the ballpark."

He stared at her gravely. "I hope not. Though, come to think of it, that would be just like you, honey."

She laughed at him and led the way out of the room. "Don't give me that look, Jared Pierce. You already knew it would never be boring."

"I did say that, didn't I?" He nodded and sighed,

then slung his arm around her shoulders to pull her close again.

It could never be boring being married to Jared, either, she thought. Not when their calling led them forward to new questions and challenges. Not when their love seemed to grow deeper and richer each day. Not when they had children to raise, whom they would teach to honor and love this wide world God had created, and to live each day with trust and faith in His Word.

* * * * *

Dear Reader,

More than twenty years ago, my wife, Johnnie, and I invited a young couple to our home after a service. They were speakers during Christian Focus Week at the university where I was teaching. After we had cake and coffee, I asked them, "How did you meet and decide to get married?"

Their answer is the basis of *Heaven Sent Husband*. It is the only one of my 186 novels that is based on a personal testimony. The novel sounds wildly improbable, a plot that I would never dream up— but it is true.

We were stunned by the faith of the young woman who risked humiliation but obeyed God blindly. All of us should have that kind of faith—but few of us do.

The real Ketura and Jared have been serving as medical missionaries for the past twenty years.

Gilbert Morris

Love Inspired®

PROTECTED HEARTS

BY

BONNIE K. WINN

When her husband and child were murdered,
Emma Perry lost her faith—and her identity. Then
she started a new life in Rosewood, Texas, where the
caring community helped her regain her faith and
introduced her to Seth McAllister, her embittered
neighbor who was also struggling to overcome a
tragedy. Together, Seth and Emma began to open
their hearts to love, just as the still-obsessed killer
picks up Emma's trail....

Don't miss PROTECTED HEARTS
On sale May 2005

Available at your favorite retail outlet.

A SHELTERING LOVE

BY

TERRI REED

Claire Wilcox sensed there was more to Nick Andrews
than met the eye. The handsome stranger who'd
saved her life twice was running from something.
Claire knew all about running—she'd been a runaway
herself. As Nick helped Claire repair the damages to
the teen center she'd established, he found himself
longing to forge a relationship with Claire...and
the God he'd shut out of his heart.

Don't miss A SHELTERING LOVE
On sale May 2005

Available at your favorite retail outlet.